# "You shouldn't be marrying Giles Lessing."

"Really," Lucy responded angrily to Matt's impertinence. "You've got your nerve coming round here to tell me what I should or shouldn't be doing! You see yourself as God's gift, don't you, and I'm a challenge. I'm the woman who ran away."

"He'll stifle you," Matt continued, ignoring her outburst.

"I'll survive. I want security and the cherishing that Giles gives me. I know what you want with me and I don't think you would do me any good."

"Compared to life with Giles," Matt commented dryly, "I don't have much to offer. You would be taking a chance."

"More like a leap in the dark!" Lucy threw back at him, frightened by Matt's nearness.

"But, it's me you want."

Matt's quiet words silenced her. When he came purposefully toward her she couldn't step back. Oh, Lucy fumed, he wasn't playing fair!

**Jane Donnelly**, a former journalist, lives in a picture-perfect cottage just outside Stratford-upon-Avon with her daughter and their assortment of pets. She has written everything from short stories to movie scripts and has developed into a prolific author of warmhearted romance novels since she started to write for Harlequin in 1968. She finds her writer's life immensely satisfying, loves the excuse to travel, and still has a reporter's instinct for gathering news and scribbling down notes, which she later uses in her books.

## Books by Jane Donnelly

Don't miss any of our special offers. Write to us at the following address for information on our newest releases.

Harlequin Reader Service
901 Fuhrmann Blvd., P.O. Box 1397, Buffalo, NY 14240
Canadian address: P.O. Box 603,
Fort Erie, Ont. L2A 5X3

# No Place to Run

## Jane Donnelly

# Harlequin Books

TORONTO • NEW YORK • LONDON
AMSTERDAM • PARIS • SYDNEY • HAMBURG
STOCKHOLM • ATHENS • TOKYO • MILAN

Original hardcover edition published in 1987
by Mills & Boon Limited

ISBN 0-373-02906-3

Harlequin Romance first edition May 1988
Second printing May 1988

# CHAPTER ONE

LUCY GILLINGHAM picked up the mail in the hall that Wednesday morning, sorted the letters for her father and mother, left them on the hall table and carried her own out to her car with her.

With a few minutes to spare she drove out of the garage, then stopped the car and opened her letters. Two were from local friends, congratulations cards 'wishing you both happiness', and there was a letter from a girl who hadn't yet heard about the engagement. Newsy chat, and she wanted to know, 'Is it still Giles?'

The last envelope contained neither card nor letter, just a magazine cutting that fell from her nerveless fingers. It was the picture of herself and Giles at that charity do last month, and written in black felt-tip beneath it, 'So that's where you've been hiding'.

The shock of it hit Lucy like a slap across the face. She sagged back in the driving seat, staring at the cutting that had fluttered under the glove compartment as if it was poisonous. Which, indeed, it could well turn out to be.

Then her mind jerked into action. Who else could have sent it? Someone who hadn't been in touch for a while? A little joke from an old friend? Maybe there *was* a letter. But the envelope was empty, her name and address written in the same handwriting that she didn't recognise, and the date stamp smudged so that she had no idea where or when it was posted.

Of course she knew who had sent it. And now he knew

who she was. Cindy Gill, she had told him, Lucinda Gillingham wasn't far from that. There was no mistake about the photograph, which was too damned lifelike, and she was wearing the Victorian keeper ring, the golden buckle: that showed clearly, too; Matt had seen her wearing it. There were plenty of keeper rings about but it was part of the proof that this was the girl he had met on Strona.

She locked her fingers together to stop them shaking. The keeper was the only ring she was wearing. Giles was giving her her engagement ring on Saturday. Dear God, *Giles*!

Matt had nothing to do with Giles. It was another girl, another life. But now Matt had found her and she had to keep him away or explain him, and keeping him away might be easier than explaining, if she could only find him. How could she start on that? Matthew Lomas of no fixed address. He had her address, which would have been child's play with the information in the caption, and this cutting was for openers, that was for sure. There would be more.

She closed her eyes and she heard him laughing. She knew her father would be coming out of the house any minute, and her reflection in the driving mirror looked distraught so that even her father, not an observant man so far as she was concerned, was going to ask, 'Are you all right?'

She turned on the ignition and put the car into gear very carefully. She could have an accident, shaken up like this. She had to go steady, to get to the office and carry on normally, and when she was less panicky decide what was to be done. But she sat in the office car park for another five minutes, pretending to read a report, before she felt up to walking in.

The *Edgeford Herald* was a giveaway weekly paper, its staff housed upstairs in the local office of the old and well-established *Staffordshire Evening Chronicle*. Lucy's five workmates were there when she arrived. Colleagues and friends, especially Jackie Allen, a petite, pert and pretty girl of Lucy's own age. As Lucy had landed one of the most eligible bachelors around, the least she could do for her best friend, Jackie had declared, was choose her for bridesmaid and see that there was a sexy and single best man.

Jackie was already seated the other side of the large working table she shared with Lucy, and that was covered with sheets of next week's paper with possible sizes of ads, some filled, some marked with queries. Jackie greeted Lucy, as she had done yesterday morning.

'Well, has Giles picked his best man yet?'

'Not yet.'

It was all Lucy could do to smile as she hung her scarlet linen jacket on the hat rack in the corner. There was a memo on her scribbling pad. She saw it from across the room and came towards it frowning, reading, 'Matthew phoned'. Only when she sat down and picked it up it said, 'Flatters phoned'. That was a hairdressing salon, regular advertisers; Lucy handled their account. It didn't look at all like Matthew and she had to stop this.

She lifted the phone and dialled their number and spoke to Karl, who gave her next week's special offers. 'Oh, and by the way, congrats,' he added chirpily.

'Thank you.' There had been no public announcement yet but the news had spread on the local grapevine, and if a stranger came into town and asked after Lucy somebody would tell him before long that she had just got engaged to Giles Lessing, Sir George's son.

She could imagine Matt's sardonic grin. She had said

she was a hard-up working girl. Well, she *was* a working girl, and she had no idea how he would react, to her engagement or to anything else. All she knew for sure was that she would see him or hear from him very soon, and when she put down the phone and it rang again immediately she nearly leapt out of the chair.

'My, you're jumpy this morning.' Kathleen Jackson, plump and matronly head of the department, smiled. 'Not getting wedding jitters already?' Lucy pretended to join in the laughter. She could have called on any of them for help in any way, but how could she explain Matt Lomas to them when she couldn't explain him to herself? Nobody could help her. She was cornered, and all she could do was wait for his next move.

Right now everybody seemed to have marriage in mind. Kathleen came back from the Wednesday morning conference to say that they wanted a picture of Lucy and Giles. 'Our ad-girl weds local tycoon.' Well, Giles was a small tycoon and almost everybody who got the giveaway paper pushed through their letter box had heard of Lessing Electronics, and Sir George was chairman of the district council.

'Do you have one?' Kathleen asked.

There were plenty of snaps but the only professional photograph was the one that had caused all the trouble, and if Lucy never saw that again it would be too soon. 'We don't have anything that would print,' she said.

She got through the day on tenterhooks, picking at her lunchtime salad and letting Jackie chatter on. Jackie was sitting with her back to the window while, outside, the square of the little town was filled with the stalls of a Wednesday market.

A man walked in the crowds in the sunshine, tall and with dark curly hair, and Lucy couldn't take her eyes off him. She stared so that Jackie stopped talking and stared, too, first at Lucy and then turning to see what Lucy saw.

He had gone, round that stall over there, and if Lucy jumped up and ran she might catch him. She needed to catch him and talk to him, only it probably was not Matt. Like the writing on the pad she was seeing him in everything, and she wasn't sure that her legs would carry her.

'What's the matter?' Jackie leaned anxiously across the table. 'You look as if you'd seen a ghost.'

Lucy said, 'I thought it was somebody I knew but it wasn't,' and Jackie went off on another track, asking, 'Do you believe in ghosts?'

'No.' Lucy forked up half a dozen baked beans and made herself swallow them, thinking, but I believe in haunting. Ever since I opened that envelope this morning I've been haunted by Matt Lomas, and it wouldn't surprise me to look up now and see him beside me.

All day he haunted her. She had appointments during the afternoon, visiting shops, a factory and an office, and more than once she thought she glimpsed him. But always when she looked again there was either nobody there or someone with very little resemblance to Matt. After she had come home, all the time she was waiting for the phone to ring. Giles was collecting her at seven, but even under the running water of the shower her ears were straining for the sound of a ringing bell.

Hearing Matt's voice would be traumatic, but it would mean that she had made contact. If he rang now she could arrange to meet him tomorrow. Until she did see him she couldn't decide about Giles. Giles might have to be told and then he would ask questions and God knew what he'd make of the answers.

But there was no phone call. Giles arrived promptly and she ran out of the house as soon as she heard his car. Sinking into the seat beside the well-built pleasant-faced man she was safe for a while. 'Where are we going?' she asked.

'I thought a meal at home. You look tired.' Her eyes were large, tip-tilted, fringed with dark lashes, but tonight they were heavy-lidded and against her mane of copper hair her skin was drained of colour. 'If the work's getting too much for you,' he said solicitously, 'hand in your notice. You won't be doing it much longer anyway.'

Her job was hardly a great career, although she enjoyed it, and if she married Giles she would have a full-time job as his wife. If she married him. She loved him, she wanted to marry him, but suddenly there was this shadow between them.

I'll tell him tonight, she vowed. Enough to prepare him. That is the least I can do, although I would give ten years of my life never to set eyes on Matt Lomas again.

Giles's penthouse apartment in his parents' home could be reached by the main staircase, but usually he used the narrower stairs at the back of the house, which ended now in the spacious hall-entrance.

The big living-room had been planned by a top designer. It was contemporary, comfortable and very stylish. In the dining section a dark mahogany table was laid for two, food ready for the serving. 'Drink?' Giles was already pouring two pale sherries into two slender glasses, and she said, 'Please,' needing something to boost her courage.

He handed her a glass and she looked into his light grey eyes and remembered eyes that were dark as pitch.

I must tell him, she kept telling herself, but she couldn't think how to start. 'When I went away in May I met this man and I'm expecting him to turn up any time now.' Giles would wait, not bothered until she went on. 'And he could make things difficult because——' It was what would have to come after 'because' that was the trouble.

They helped themselves to gazpacho followed by hot salmon steaks and salad and then a lemon sorbet. They drank chilled wine and Lucy took more than usual. The food she hardly tasted, and the wine didn't help. They were draining their coffee cups before she blurted out, 'How many girls were there before me?'

Giles was talking about her joining the golf club and he needed a moment to adjust. Then he shrugged, dismissing her predecessors. 'None that mattered.'

'You've never asked me about my past.'

'Because I've known you all your life.' He thought she was joking. 'So I know all your secrets, my darling.'

He stood up and lifted her to her feet and kissed her tenderly. She needed her wits about her; the wine had been a mistake. She was in no state now to start explaining and excusing herself. 'I think I should go home,' she said.

He was still holding her in his arms and now he kissed her again, deeper and urgently. 'Not yet,' he whispered, and he was drawing her towards the open door of the bedroom. Maybe she should have gone because letting him love her should prove that she belonged to him and to nobody else. But she found herself pulling away.

He thought it was a playful tussle and smiled and said, 'You are home,' but then, seeing the whitening of her lips and the tension of her body, 'Darling, what *is* the matter?'

She said miserably, 'I'm tired, it's been a long day.' It was a rotten excuse, and she knew that Giles was undecided whether he should cuddle and coax her or accept gracefully that she was not in a loving mood.

She should have been. She should have had nothing on her mind but how much she wanted this man she was going to marry, and she could have burst into tears thinking what a mess it all was. He was not trying to draw her towards the bedroom now. He was looking at her like a doctor. 'You do look all in. If this goes on you really must quit your job.'

'I'm sorry,' she whispered.

'Not to worry. Come on, then.' She sensed his injured pride although he hid it well enough. On the way home he turned on the car radio and when they drew up in front of her home he kissed her and said, 'I've got to go up to Manchester tomorrow and I'll probably stay overnight. Now take it easy, darling. I'll see you on Saturday; it's going to be a special day for us.' She was getting her ring on Saturday and the day should be special.

'I love you,' she said.

'Of course you do.' He smiled and kissed her again and drove away as she put her key in the lock. The door of her father's study was open. As she crossed the hall Laurence Gillingham, dandified in a dark blue smoking jacket and smoking a cigar, came to stand in the lighted doorway.

'Had a good evening?' he called.

'Splendid.'

'Good, good.'

If Giles chucks me, she thought, you'll never forgive me for letting your rich son-in-law get away.

Her head tossed on the pillow that night until it began

to ache, and she fell asleep trying to still the throbbing.

There was nothing that mattered in the mail next morning. It will be a phone call, she thought. He'll ring my home. If he rings tonight I shall make it plain that I don't ever want to see him again and that what happened on Strona meant nothing at all.

She ate alone that evening, settling for a bowl of soup. The phone did ring twice, and each time her heart seemed to stop beating and then race so fast that when she picked up the receiver she felt physically ill. Both callers were cut off with the same excuse, 'I'm just on my way out in a terrible rush,' but at eight o'clock she was still waiting and listening.

This was pathetic. She couldn't go on like this. But when it rang again it panicked her again and she decided, if this isn't him that's it for tonight. I'm getting out of the house. I'm going spare sitting here, sweating it out.

It was Aunt Maud, who understood how busy she was with just getting engaged but wanted to know how things were going and what was she doing this evening? 'Not a lot right now,' said Lucy.

'Then come and have a bite of supper,' said Aunt Maud, 'I've got something to tell you.'

She had probably been to another auction sale and Lucy hoped she wasn't thinking about wedding presents, but she said, 'Yes, all right. I'll walk down.'

She heard the phone ringing yet again as she shut the front door. She rooted in her bag for her keys, fumbled with the lock and ran down the hall to answer it. As she put her hand out the ringing stopped, but she picked up the phone and listened to the dialling sound. Then she slammed it down again and leaned against the wall, feeling wrung out. At this rate she'd soon be a nervous wreck and Giles would decide she was unbalanced as well as frigid.

She walked down the hill into the town, the breeze lifting her red hair and cooling her flushed cheeks. The door of Aunt Maud's house was open, and she walked in. Usually she called, 'I'm here,' but tonight she came in quietly. There was no one in the parlour. It was cool in the fading light, and Lucy stood before the old mirror smoothing down her hair with both hands. She didn't want Aunt Maud seeing her looking as though someone had been chasing her.

This old mirror reflected, as always, not quite as other mirrors did. In its mottled surface her face was always misty and dreamlike. Tonight it was all eyes—she *looked* haunted—and through the windows behind her in the green of the gardens, something moved like a ghost.

Her mouth fell open and she almost tripped into the fireplace, peering into the mirror as though what was happening was in there. Then she turned her head slowly, looking sidelong into the garden.

Of course she wasn't seeing ghosts. He *was* in Aunt Maud's garden, and now he was just outside the window, looking in at her. Oh, he was real enough. The dark hair springing back from the wide forehead, the dark eyes and the long mouth. He wore a light-coloured T-shirt and jeans over the lean body she knew so well, and at the sight of him in the hard flesh rage boiled in her. How dare he send anonymous messages worrying her out of her mind, coming down here and telling Aunt Maud lord-knew what?

She was so furious, she was shaking. She could hardly pull back the window latch and push up the bottom half of the old-fashioned sashcord window to lean out and snarl, 'What the hell do you think you're doing here?'

He sat on the windowsill and swung long legs into the room, landing as lithely as a cat, and she jumped away as if he would scald her if he touched her, although she should have had the sense to shove him back. This was breaking and entering. He'd make a good cat burglar. She remembered how surefooted he was, scaling rocks, reaching down to haul her up beside him.

'I've come for my wife, of course,' he said.

# CHAPTER TWO

Lucy had been looking for peace and quiet when she went to the island. As long as she could remember her father and mother had led a cat-and-dog life. They were a popular pair. He was a lawyer, holding the years at bay with just a slightly thickening waistline and a distinguished touch of grey at the temples. Sylvia was willowy, blonde and beautiful enough to have a string of admirers, and they kept up the sham of their marriage because it suited them both.

They did most of their rowing in private. Over the years their daughter had tried to shut her ears to raised voices and slamming doors, but they made her wary of marriage. Since she was seventeen she had been notching up proposals and propositions without seriously considering any of them.

At twenty-three she was strikingly attractive; with parents as good-looking as hers it would have been odd if she had been plain. In May she was dating Giles, but only as a close friend, and a particularly ferocious set-to at home, when her father found several of her mother's unpaid bills in a bureau, suddenly hit a nerve and triggered a migraine.

She had to get away. 'If I don't have a break from them,' she told Aunt Maud, 'there'll be murder done. A lighthouse would be nice. Or a trip up the Amazon where no one could get hold of me.' Suddenly it came to her. 'How about Strona?'

That made Aunt Maud sit up and purse her lips. 'You'd be on your own there all right. Why don't you find a comfortable hotel?'

'I'll take Strona,' Lucy said.

'Then I should take a good book,' said Aunt Maud.

When Giles suggested he might manage a few days off to go with her, Lucy said, 'I'd like that, but some other time. Right now I need to get away from everybody.'

'Even from me?' He was hurt because he thought their relationship was coming along nicely, but she had told him,

'You'd hate it. It's dead rugged. All I'm going to do is sleep, and walk and swim if the weather's good. If it isn't I'll sit in the window and watch the sheep and wish I hadn't gone.'

'And think of me?'

'Of course.'

He wondered if she was going to prove to him that he would miss her; she was adamant that she didn't want company. Aunt Maud phoned to check that the cottage was empty, and Lucy moved quickly, leaving for Strona within the week.

The last time she had visited the island had been over fifteen years ago, after Aunt Maud went touring the Scottish isles, fell in love with them, and bought herself a holiday home that was certainly going cheap.

She had described it in glowing terms and persuaded Lucy's parents, with Lucy, to take the trip up with her for a week's family holiday. It had to be a week because the ferry only ran on Saturdays, doing a round trip that meant touching down at Strona in the morning and again in the evening.

When the Gillinghams had disembarked at the landing bay it was not a promising start. They had difficulty persuading Sylvia to get out at all. A drizzle of rain had made the broken stones of the jetty and patches of sea moss covering most of them treacherously slippy, and the only buildings in the little harbour were ruins half buried in the sands.

Sylvia had been in a state of shock for a good ten minutes while Laurence and Lucy carried the baggage and Maud strode on, waving a walking stick, naming the birds that were wheeling overhead, although Lucy was sure that the one she called a kittiwake wasn't.

'Where is the cottage?' Laurence had wanted to know.

It was not far from the shore. One storey and built of grey granite. Maud had produced a massive key, opened the door with a flourish and stood back.

'Now what do you think of that?'

Lucy had thought it was like something out of a book, rugged and old, with a big stone fireplace and black pots. Her mother had given a croak and then just stood there, swaying slightly.

'Where is everyone?' her father had asked. They had only passed a few sheep.

Aunt Maud had said, 'Indoors, I should think, on a day like this. There are more cottages, holiday homes. Before the clearances, of course, there were crofters, but then the land was given over to the sheep.'

'What clearances?' Sylvia was finding her voice while Maud applied a match to the dark mass in the fireplace from which clouds of smoke promptly belched. She had said scornfully,

'What did they teach you in that fancy finishing school of yours? The clearances of 1850, of course, when the islanders were forced out of their homes and shipped off across the Atlantic. A very nasty business. Whipped on to the boats some of them were.'

'You mean they didn't want to go?' Sylvia had been incredulous. 'I'd have thought they'd have been fighting to get off. I surely will.'

She had been as good as her word. When the little ship had come into sight again that evening she had been on the jetty frantically signalling it in. It had been a depressing day and Sylvia was not facing a night, let alone a week, stuck in Maud's foul little cottage on the godforsaken island.

For once she and Laurence had agreed with each other. Maud had admitted that she had bought the cottage when the sun was shining, but she herself would stay because the weather was going to improve. They had all trooped down to the deserted landing bay, but Lucy had hung back when her father called, 'Come on, Lucy.'

'I want to stay,' she'd said, and they'd left her with hardly a backwards glance, ducking undercover down to the saloon deck as soon as they had stepped on board, although Lucy and Aunt Maud had waved in the rain until the little steamer was almost out of sight.

In spite of Maud Beale's premonition the weather had stayed wretched, but they had set off most days squelching over the rough turf, climbing the gentler hills. They had spent time on the beach, among the ghost village that had been fishermen's cottages until the soft sands had covered them.

At night, by the peat fire and the light of oil lamps, Maud had told Lucy tales of the isles. Some were history, some she had made up as she went along—she had an imagination that had always run to the weird and wonderful—and Lucy had listened entranced.

On the following Saturday as they had waited on the jetty, still in the rain, Aunt Maud had said, 'It wasn't too bad, was it?' and Lucy had replied fervently, 'It was lovely. Can we come again?'

By then Maud Beale's rheumatism had been making itself felt and she had given a non-committal grunt. Nobody had mentioned Strona to Sylvia for a long time after that, and when Lucy said in May that she was going up there for a few days a look of horror came into her mother's eyes.

'Does Maud still have that hovel? I used to have nightmares I was a castaway on that island.'

'I rather liked it,' Lucy said.

When she stepped ashore this time the sun was shining. Not much else had changed, except that drifting sands had altered the pattern of the ghost village on the beach. Others got off the boat, too, some with binoculars, obviously bird watchers, and a group with boxes of provisions. Sunshine made all the difference, and she opened the door of the cottage with a little nostalgic thrill.

It looked exactly the same as fifteen years ago: a wooden table, dresser and chairs, a small Calor gas cooker and a sink up by the big old fireplace, and a bedroom half divided into a small bathroom.

She had brought a sleeping bag which she dropped on the bed, and then she unpacked clothes and the bag containing her week's supply of food. The cottage was clean. Sometimes it was let through an agent. A fire was laid with kindling and a little coal, and there were peat-squares stacked by the fireplace. If the weather held camping-out would be fun, because goodness knows it was rugged.

Lucy was wearing jeans and trainers and a scarlet and white striped shirt. She didn't need to bother changing and within minutes she was outside the cottage, looking all ways, deciding where to go, filled with the elation of freedom.

She could remember exploring the little bays and caves with Aunt Maud, mostly staying on the lower slopes, but now she could go where she chose, and if she was unlucky enough to have an accident there were others on the island. She spied tents pitched and she passed a thatched cottage with a door ajar and a curl of smoke rising from the chimney.

She was looking for the singing cave. Some of the

caves were honeycombed with wind tunnels and Aunt Maud had taken her into one that made echoing melodies when you hummed a tune or sang a few notes. Lucy had trilled away, and in her child's mind the music of the cave had been pure magic.

In the singing cave was the ring of rock, a hole in the rock through which a couple joined hands, and that had been considered as binding as any marriage vows. Aunt Maud had shown it to her. She had stood on tiptoe to stretch her arm through, and Aunt Maud had chuckled and said, 'Mind it now, you never know what will grab you,' and Lucy had squealed and jumped back.

She reached another bay, walking along the beach, scrambling over the rocks. The sun sparkled on the water and there was a sprinkling of holidaymakers. It was very different from how it had looked under grey skies through the eyes of a child. Deliberately she shut out the others, intent on retracing and recalling the steps she had taken years ago. One cave did seem to stir a memory. Light filtered in, and among the boulders was a cleft rock, the fissure wide enough to take clasped hands.

When she called, 'Hello!' it echoed and she was almost sure this was the cave. She called again and listened again, and then she went to the split rock and put her hand through. At the same moment she was aware of being watched by a man standing in the mouth of the cave.

'Lost somebody?' He strolled in. 'I don't think you're going to find them in there.' She jerked back so fast that the back of her hand scraped on the rough surface.

It was absurd, calling to nobody and shaking hands with rocks, and she didn't need to explain, but she said, 'You don't know the story of the singing cave and the ring of rock?'

'I know it.' She was rather surprised it was not an

Aunt Maud invention.

'Well I think this is the cave.' She was certain now that she had been brought here, even when he said 'No.'

Still, the story was genuine. Aunt Maud had just put it in a handy setting. 'I could take you to it,' he offered, and, because she had nothing else to do with what was left of the day and she would like to find the authentic article, she thanked him.

Out of the cave in brighter light she saw him more clearly. He was tall, broad-shouldered and narrow-hipped, and as they turned to face each other she thought his was a face that might have been carved, with its high Red Indian cheekbones and the strong hard planes of the mouth and jaw. Late twenties, early thirties, tough. She asked, 'Do you live here?'

'On the island? Nobody does. There are a few holiday homes, a few under canvas or sleeping on the beach while the weather's good. Where are you?'

'In a house by the landing bay.'

'On your own?'

It might not be smart to declare yourself a girl alone but she said, 'Yes.'

'I'm Matt,' he said. 'Matthew Lomas.' He waited for her name. There was no reason not to tell him but she heard herself say 'Cindy Gill,' and perhaps he noticed her hesitation because he left it at that.

'Follow me,' he said. They climbed the cliffs; the sun was on her face and hands, and the warm wind smelt of the sea. No wonder Aunt Maud settled for a cave down there, she thought, it's a rough old scramble. She panted, 'You're sure you know where we're going?'

He wore an open-necked check shirt. His skin was tanned to mahogany and she was sure he was the same dark tan all over. When he grinned it took some of the hardness from his face and she began to laugh because she felt like laughing. 'In the old days,' he said, 'they used to get the whole wedding party up here.'

'I hope it kept fine for them.'

'Not often. You don't know how lucky you are, getting weather like this.'

'I do. Last time I was here it never stopped raining. Everything looks different in the sunshine.'

He reached down to drag her up, and as she landed beside him she was sharply aware of his closeness and the strength of his hand around her fingers. 'In here.' He still held her hand as they squirmed through a narrow gap off the ledge of rock into a cave.

'Helloo,' she carolled into the darkness. 'Anybody home?' The echoes harmonised.

It was a small cave but there was enough light to see once her eyes got used to it, and she peered around for the ring of rock. 'This one,' he said.

The rock did have an almost round hole right through the middle and she wondered it hadn't been carted off to some museum or other. It was thrilling to see and touch and imagine lovers coming here and committing themselves to each other with a clasp of hands. If somebody hummed a few bars of music they could have had a choir of echoes thrown in.

'I thought my aunt might have made up the story.' She ran her fingers round the rough edge of rock. 'She told it to me when we were here years and years ago. She does have a lively imagination but I'm glad it's true. Did they always get married that way on this island?'

As he knew where the ring was, he might know more about it—and he did. 'For a few years before the clearances the young folk were forbidden to marry unless they emigrated, so they married with the ring of rock. Like gypsies jumping hand in hand over the campfire.'

He could be a gypsy, dark in the shadows.

She said, 'Well, thank you for bringing me here,' and

she put her hand through because it was irresistible, gasping when his fingers closed over hers. He loosed her within seconds and they both laughed and the singing cave took up their laughter. Outside the sun was still so bright that she had to close her eyes against it.

From then on a magic seemed to seize her, as if she had fallen under the spell of the island. In Matt she found a fantastic companion. He took her walking, climbing, swimming, and everything had a sharper edge, as if she had been only half alive before.

After a shower of rain there was a rainbow, Lucy had never seen colours like it. And then the sun came out again and, as they lay on the rocks, it was so hot that she was glad she had brought suntan oil, although she had only tossed it into her case as an afterthought. Matt oiled her with slow, sensuous hands; it was bliss, but there was no urgency in his attitude. He thought she was attractive but he never pressured her.

That first night they went back to her cottage and ate bread and cheese and a tin of ham from her store cupboard, and afterwards he asked, 'May I stay?'

But when she said, 'I'd rather you didn't,' he said, 'Fair enough. I'll see you tomorrow.' They parted with no hassle at all.

He came, mid-morning, bringing fruit and a packet of biscuits and a replacement tin of corned beef, so he had stores somewhere. Nights he must go back to a cottage or a tent or a cave. Once a couple of men were climbing a hill, coming towards them, and he drew her back and down in the heather.

She said nothing. She lay, looking at him quizzically, until they were well past. Then she asked, 'Friends of yours?'

'Yes. Do you want to meet them?'

'I don't think so.'

She didn't want to meet anyone else. Matt was all the

companionship she needed. Theirs was a relationship without past or future, but she waited for him each morning with an absolute certainty that he would come.

On their second day they walked for miles and ended in a cove where she flopped down on the sands. She had a swimsuit under a dress but when he said, 'Coming in?' she shook her head.

'Give me a break.'

He seemed tireless. He left her and began to climb the rocks, swift and surefooted, and she watched lazily. By the time he was at the top, silhouetted against the skyline, she was sitting bolt upright, shading her eyes with her hand because it was dawning on her what might come next.

Before she could shout, which probably wouldn't have stopped him, he had dived from what seemed to be an incredible height. It was a perfect dive and he surfaced and took off in a strong fast crawl. He knew exactly what he was doing although he had given her a heart-stopping moment.

Lucy watched him swimming out. He was not showing off. He was superbly fit, a powerhouse of energy, a man to reckon with. And for all she knew a bigamist or a bank robber on the run, because she never learned much about him.

She didn't tell him much either. She told him nothing; he didn't ask any questions. There seemed to be an unspoken agreement that neither pried, and it suited her; she didn't want to swap pasts and backgrounds. When she stepped on that ferry on Saturday, Cindy would cease to exist.

But they were not like strangers. They talked easily and the silences were natural; it was as though they had known each other for years, so that the here and now could be savoured and nothing else mattered.

When he came out of the sea, shaking water all over

her, she asked, 'Do you always jump off cliffs?'

'It's safe there. There are no underwater rocks.'

'I was thinking of walking in,' she said.

She waded into the waves. It was bitterly cold and she shivered, but ducked and swam and he swam alongside her. In Giles's heated pool they often swam together, more or less matched for speed and stamina, but she would be no match for Matt at this game. Not that they were competing.

Out in the bay they clambered on to a rock and she dived back in from there. She dived higher in the days that followed but never, of course, from anywhere near the top of the cliff. If I stayed all summer I might manage that, she thought, but she couldn't stay and she didn't say it.

Friday brought the shower of rain and the rainbow and then the sunshine again, and she lay with her chin on the edge of a rock pool. The sunlight made green glittering patterns from weed and sand. 'It's like an old mirror,' said Lucy. Like the mirror in Aunt Maud's parlour. 'I've got this old aunt,' she began to tell him, looking down into the rock pool. 'Well, she's a great-aunt actually—she's well into her seventies—and she's got an old green mirror in a green room. I used to think it was a witch's glass when I was a kid and that if you stared into it hard enough and wished hard you'd get your wish. But it didn't work often. I had better luck telling Aunt Maud what I was wishing for. She was always a great one for calling up the magic. A bit of a witch herself.'

Once started on Aunt Maud she went on; he finished oiling her and lay beside her, smiling because Aunt Maud was a colourful character. 'She loves auction sales. Her house is jam-packed with stuff because she swears she gets the vibes, knows what's been cherished and is crying out for a good home. She lives in what used to be the old school. The stone arch over the entrance is carved with 'Remember thy maker in the days of thy youth'. She lives in what was the headmistress's house, and then there was just one big schoolroom. It's well over fifty years since it was used for that. Now they have jumble sales and church bazaars and sometimes a disco in it. The rest of the time it's full of junk. A couple of years ago she took in some art students and they painted some murals for her which look as though they just chucked pots of paint at the walls. I think they did. They left at the end of their course and she still won't admit it was a mistake.'

One tale led to another and when she finished they were both laughing.

'You should write a book,' he said.

'Who'd believe me?'

'What do you do for a living?'

Talking about Aunt Maud hadn't mattered, but she didn't want to talk about herself. All that would come round again soon enough so she said, deliberately offhand, 'I'm a hard-up working girl. I work in an office. Nothing exciting.' She jerked herself upright, looking across the beach at a couple who were walking along the sea's edge, the woman in a bright yellow halter-neck dress, and, changing the subject, 'Isn't it an incredible week for May? Wouldn't it be heaven if we had a scorching summer?'

'You're leaving tomorrow?'

'Yes.'

'That doesn't give us much time,' he said, putting a hand on her bare shoulder, and she felt the shock of it down to her fingertips and toes, because this touch was different.

Or was it? Hadn't every touch been like this? Holding hands, walking, swimming in deep water and lacing cold wet limbs. Hadn't it been lovemaking almost from that

first morning? Although he had said 'See you tomorrow,' each night, and she had slept alone, each night she
had been surprised when he went.

Now time had almost run out. They went back to the
cottage after the sun had set and a little wind had blown
up from the sea, and she brought out all that was left of
her stores. Most mornings Matt had arrived with a bag
of something or other, so there was a mixed collection on
the wooden-topped table.

They opened the tins and tipped out the contents and
Matt made a ceremony of uncorking a bottle of wine and
setting it in the middle of the table to breathe. Lucy
pottered around barefoot, pretending she was preparing
a party. Doing silly things like cutting up tinned
pineapple into bites and making patterns with a bag of
crisps and slab of cheese. And they lit a fire.

She hadn't bothered with that before, the weather was
so warm, but tonight Matt coaxed a flame from the
kindling, sitting cross-legged and blowing until the peat
caught, and when it was dark they lit the lamps.

The windows were deep-set. Other nights she had
looked out at the stars but this was the first time that the
wind was blowing hard enough to bring up the sand in a
faint swirling cloud.

When the meal was over she stood at the window and
thought, this is how it must have started for those
cottages on the beach. A little sand at first. Matt was just
behind her; when she swayed back a fraction she was
leaning against him.

She was caught in the spell of the past. This house had
hardly changed since the clearances. The lamps and the
furniture would have been the same and the peat fire in
the hearth, and she half turned her head to rest her cheek
against the man's shoulder. She had married him by the
ring of rock; other lovers had gone back to cottages on
Strona—maybe to this one—and considered themselves

one flesh until death did them part. His lips brushed the nape of her neck and she turned to him, putting up her arms and pulling his face down to hers. She felt his smile and the urgency of his body. The wind howled in the chimney. Maybe the ferry would not sail tomorrow and she would have to stay.

But not for long. The ferry would come and she would go, and Matt was no dream lover. He was a virile man of flesh and blood and, back home after tonight, what would she do if she found she was pregnant?

That shattered the fantasy. What an idiot she was to be playing with fire like this.

'Please, let's wait until we're away from here. I think it would be wonderful, but not here. I'm scared to take this kind of risk. Oh, *please* don't.'

He could force her, no doubt of that. They were alone. Nobody would hear, nobody would know. And she would get most of the blame because she had been criminally provocative and daft as a brush. When she realised he was not angry—his expression was one of rueful amusement—she sniffed back the tears, going limp with relief, swallowing because her throat seemed to have closed up as her nerves had tightened like piano wires.

'All right,' he said. 'Don't look so scared, you're not cornered. We'll wait ...' She had hiccups now '... so long as you don't turn me out tonight. I'll settle for the rug in front of the fire.'

Oddly the hiccups helped. She sounded so silly burping away, and now she knew she was safe she began to smile. 'Sorry about this—as well.'

'They say a shock's the cure.' He smiled and they were joking and it was good again.

'Please, no shocks. I'll hold my breath.' She did, clapping a hand over her mouth until the hiccups subsided.

Now he seemed more a protector than a threat and she said, 'I wouldn't dream of turning you out.' There were sheepskin rugs but the stone floor would make a hard mattress. 'I'll take the sleeping bag and you're welcome to the rest of the bed.'

'Thank you.'

In the little bedroom she squirmed into the sleeping bag zipping it up to her chin and from the doorway Matt said, 'An all-over chastity belt, that's protection. Shall I turn out the lamps or are you scared of the dark too?'

'Who, me? Not at all.' The acrid smell of oil lingered as he came through the darkness, the bed creaking as he lay down beside her, slipping an arm under her head.

It was comforting to curl close. Those few moments when every nerve and muscle had been at panic pitch had drained her strength, so that this quiet embrace seemed almost like the ebbtide of passion. She could almost believe they had made ecstatic love and were now drifting to sleep.

'Will you come with me?' he said.

'What?' She would have been asleep in seconds.

He was looking down into her shadowed face and she could hardly keep her eyes open. 'Tomorrow, will you come with me?'

'Yes.' She nestled against him, her cheek against his chest so that she could hear his heartbeats.

She woke when he touched her. He was standing beside the bed, and it was morning because it was light. 'Hi,' she said sleepily.

He kissed her lips but as she stirred he moved away, telling her, 'I've got to collect gear. I'll be back.'

She snuggled down again for another hour or so but it wasn't easy to get back to sleep. It was Saturday, the day the ferry came. They would be expecting her back tomorrow night and she had promised Matt she would go with him. She remembered that. She had not dreamt it. But she could do no such thing.

Last night had shown how she could lose her head over him, and he was a man about whom she knew nothing. Her parents had fallen for each other at first sight. Her mother had walked down a staircase at a hunt ball and her father had said 'Who is that? I'm going to marry her.' Marry they did, six weeks later, without a thing in common but their charm and their selfishness. Lucy was going to be very sure, before she let herself fall in love, that the relationship had firmer foundations than skin-deep attraction.

Every other morning she had pottered around, blissfully contented, but this morning she packed and cleaned and rehearsed what she would say to Matt. It came to 'Goodbye. I know I said there would be an afterwards but there won't. You might have a wife and family. I'm sure there's someone waiting. And I have to go home because there are those who are waiting for me.'

But the pull between them was fierce and she hoped she could resist it when they were face to face. She looked at her small pile of luggage and wished she could pick it up and run away. She stood in the doorway, looking out to sea. There were boats out there. Sometimes motor boats came into the coves; she might hitch a lift off Strona. Although she could hardly dash around the coast trying to find an obliging crew.

But she could catch the ferry this morning when it made its stop here prior to half a dozen other islands, some with airstrips and ferries that could get her to the mainland. Or at any rate away from Matt.

She wrote a note: 'Thank you for everything. I had a lovely holiday. Good luck and goodbye, C.' and waited. If he came before the ferry she would have to tell him it was goodbye, and she was almost sure he would take it calmly.

When she thought about it, the previous night

showed that he wasn't burning up for her. He fancied her, yes, he thought they had unfinished business, and he would be puzzled and probably disappointed. But of course there were other girls for a man like him. In no way was she the right one, any more than he would be right for her once they were off the island.

He was taking his time and she was glad about that. When she saw the ferry coming she locked the door and put the note under a stone. Then she hurried to the end of the jetty where the water was deep and clear, hoping she wouldn't hear him calling her. She didn't look back until she was on board. She saw the little group that had disembarked walking along the beach, and Aunt Maud's cottage, closed and quiet, and no sign of Matt at all.

Her getaway was a panic flight. He might know someone with a boat anchored off Strona, he could come looking for her along the ferry's route, so she had to put real distance between them. As she paid for her passage, she asked the quickest way to the mainland, then sweated it out island-hopping, and only felt safe when she was hurtling along in a train that was taking her to Glasgow and a flight to Birmingham the next day.

She stayed overnight in a Glasgow hotel. A hot scented bath seemed to wash deep until all that was left of Cindy was the faint mark of the rock graze on the back of her hand. She was too tired to eat much of her evening meal and went back to her room, unaware of the glances of fellow diners, some of whom looked curiously at the tall, lovely girl, with her mane of bright coppery hair, suntanned and grave-faced, who had sat alone and left her plate almost untouched.

The hotel bedroom was impersonal but it was luxury after the cottage, and the bed was a big improvement on the sleeping bag and the ancient mattress. Last night she had slept in Matt's arms and tonight she would not think of Matt. Tomorrow she was going home. She sighed and rested her cheek against the cool pillow and fell into an exhausted sleep until the phone rang with her early morning call.

She had left her car at Birmingham and she drove herself home. Her mother and father seemed pleased to see her. 'I must say,' said Sylvia, 'you look remarkably well, considering. Will you be going up there again?'

'No,' Lucy said emphatically and Sylvia laughed.

'Well, it's done no harm. Giles rang last night to ask what time we expected you back. He sounded as if he couldn't wait. I said you'd call him.'

Lucy rang Ivory Grange, Giles's home, and Giles answered as if he was waiting for her call. 'I missed you,' he said. 'I've been lonely without you.'

'Me too,' she said. 'I missed you, too,' and she was horrified, thinking of the risks she had run. If she and Matt had been lovers she would have been racked with guilt and apprehension now. As it was she was ashamed of lying in her teeth.

'Do anything interesting?' Giles asked. 'Meet anybody?'

'Only the sheep,' she said. 'They were looking well.'

She never mentioned Matt. She said she had had a lazy week and she had been lucky in the weather. She reassured Aunt Maud that the cottage was OK and a week on her own had done her health and temper a power of good. She could hardly say, 'I met this man as soon as I got there. I know his name but he never told me anything else, although we were together every day and for one night.' So she told them what they expected to hear and nobody suspected anything because Giles Lessing was the only man in her life.

For a while she wondered if Matt might try to trace her. It worried her. From that week Giles had become more possessive and more loving—putting her on a pedestal because he tended to idealise women who mattered to him—and it would have shattered him to hear that she had been anything but alone on Strona.

But days passed and weeks merged into months. Life at home went on as usual, only now she had Giles to turn to and Matt was a dimming memory. She hadn't given him a thought in ages. Until that magazine cutting arrived; since then she had hardly thought about anything else, and now he was here.

Come for his *wife*? What sort of crazy talk was that? She said, 'That is a rotten joke.'

He smiled. She didn't know much about him but she knew without any doubt at all that he was capable of anything. 'Who's joking?' he asked.

# CHAPTER THREE

'THEN you *are* raving mad,' croaked Lucy. 'Where's Aunt Maud?' Matt jerked his head towards the door, which meant somewhere else in the house. 'What have you told her?'

'Nothing.'

'What *are* you doing here?'

She heard Aunt Maud coming, heels clattering on the flagstones of the passage from the kitchen and bangles jangling. He crossed to open the door wider and take the tray she was carrying. 'Introduced yourselves, have you?' said Aunt Maud, all smiles, so it seemed Matt hadn't told her.

She was a tall woman, her still-dark hair cut in fringe and bob, her flowing dress all colours of the rainbow, and she wore an assortment of gold chains and bangles. This room was like the rest of the house, full of clutter, and as he looked around for somewhere to deposit the tray Lucy said, 'Put it here,' taking a bowl of wax fruit and a motheaten stuffed ferret off a sidetable.

'I'm Matthew Lomas,' he said, 'and you must be Lucy Gillingham.'

She closed the window and switched on a light and decided to hear what was coming next. She could always say, 'Cindy Gill when we met before,' but she was blurting out nothing until she knew what was going on.

'Isn't she beautiful?' said Aunt Maud and Matt said, 'Unforgettable. May I call you Lucy?' Lucy's face flamed.

'What else would you call her?' said Aunt Maud merrily.

He was holding out his hand. 'How do you do, Lucy. This is a pleasure.'

'Not an unexpected one,' she muttered. She would rather have kept her hand to herself but she had to reach out, and as her fingers brushed his he caught and held them hard for a moment.

'We were both expecting you,' said Aunt Maud, 'and I want your advice.'

Lucy had felt the electricity when he touched her; she would not let that happen again. She sat down on one of the little green plush Victorian chairs and looked at Aunt Maud and sounded amused. '*My* advice? What's happened to the crystal ball and the tea leaves?'

Maud Beale's friends swore by her as a fortune teller and she usually shuffled the cards when she had any problems herself. Not that she had many. She was comfortably off and enjoying life. Lucy couldn't remember being consulted much.

'Pie?' Aunt Maud sliced into the steaming savoury pie and handed out dishes. 'Preserves, pickles, help yourselves.' She waited until they were sitting with their plates, then she said, 'Matthew wants to buy the cottage on Strona.'

'Does he now?' Lucy looked straight at him, but his face could have been a mask for all it told her. 'Why?'

The obvious answer. It was a fairly sound property and he wanted a cottage on the islands. He had been looking for some time and in the end had come back to Strona.

'What tipped the balance?' asked Lucy. 'It's hardly the pick of the islands.'

'Because Matthew's family came from Strona,' Aunt Maud explained. 'Before the clearances.'

'Really.' That could be true, but Lucy's eyebrows rose and, 'They did?' was a question.

'Don't you believe it?' he said. She shrugged.

'I find it hard to believe that your ancestors would be shifted from their land and packed on to boats, if they were anything like you.' Aunt Maud, who had just speared a pickled onion on her fork, waved it in the air.

'All that was a long time ago. The question now is, do you want to keep the cottage?'

'Me?' Lucy never wanted to see it again but she had to sound reasonable and detatched. 'Well, it isn't as though you ever go up there yourself, and how long is it since any of your friends did?' Maud Beale was as hospitable with her holiday home as she was with this house. She was always putting up friends here but Lucy couldn't remember the last time she had heard of anyone visiting Strona. She summed up, 'Nobody you know uses it. Do you want to sell?' She looked towards Matt again. 'And what are you offering?' She would be glad to see it go but if he thought he was getting it for peanuts he could think again. The figure sounded reasonable and she said, 'It's your cottage, love. It's up to you. It can't be much of an investment; I should think the lettings hardly cover the expenses.'

'I thought you might want to go up again some time,' said Aunt Maud. 'Perhaps take Giles with you. Even perhaps on your honeymoon.'

Lucy would have choked if she had been trying to eat the pie. As it was she had to gulp before she could say, 'Giles would hate it. Can you imagine him in that bathroom? It's primitive.'

Then she wished she hadn't said that, because the bathroom led off the bedroom; Matt knew them well. Aunt Maud gave a throaty chuckle, probably visualising Giles.

'He's very fastidious,' Lucy countered wildly. 'What on earth gave you the idea I'd want to take him to Strona?'

Matt had put down his plate. He was leaning forward

as if this should be interesting. Aunt Maud said, 'I know you needed a break from the family when you went up there to be on your own, but you went to make up your mind about Giles as well, didn't you?' She sounded wise and knowing, and she was usually astute. If the week had worked out as Lucy expected, she would have spent a lot of time thinking about Giles, wondering whether she was falling in love with him and he with her. As it was she had almost forgotten he existed until that morning.

'And you did make up your mind,' said Aunt Maud, with the triumph of someone who can prove her point, 'because after you came back it was all Giles, wasn't it? Nobody else for either of you after that. And now you're getting married. So I thought you might want to take him to the cottage, on a sentimental journey.'

Aunt Maud was often an embarrassment to her parents but this was the first time Lucy had wished her out of the way. 'A sentimental journey,' Matt echoed, as if he had never heard the phrase before and thought it was charming. 'If I buy the cottage you can be my guests.'

Don't play cat and mouse with me, Lucy signalled. She looked at him through narrowed eyes and she could feel her own mouth hardening. 'No need,' she said harshly. 'I wouldn't be seen dead in the place.'

She heard Aunt Maud gasp, 'Why, you sound like your mother!' Her face was bewildered, and Lucy thought wryly that if her psychic powers were real, and not all in the mind all these years, that charge of animosity must have knocked her back.

Because Lucy had wanted to hit the man. She was not a violent girl, she hated violence. Who in their right mind didn't? But he had given her three nerve-racking days and now he was laughing at her, and the strain of still not knowing how to deal with him was telling.

Aunt Maud did not need to be psychic to be shocked at

the sight of Lucy snarling at a man who seemed to be a well-mannered stranger. We must talk, Lucy thought. I must get him alone and find out just what his game is.

She drew a slow steadying breath, and pulled an apologetic grimace. 'That was an overstatement, but I don't think Giles and I will be going up there, so don't hang on to it on our account. Although, if you do decide to sell, of course you'd be getting another valuation.' Smilingly she asked Matt, 'When did you turn up with this offer?'

'Yesterday.'

'And you're hanging around, waiting for an answer?'

'That's right.'

'Where are you staying?' Somewhere else, she hoped, but it came as no surprise when Aunt Maud chipped in, 'Here.

'So the sooner you make up your mind, the sooner he'll be on his way,' said Lucy and Aunt Maud, who had quite recovered her spirits, said cheerfully,

'Not until he's finished the garden. He's cutting the lawns for me.' Her regular gardener was on a three-week holiday and the grass was growing.

'Well, that shouldn't take long,' Lucy said.

She had to stay a little while longer. A quarter of an hour should do it but in the meantime she sat there, drinking coffee and pushing her food around the plate and trying to keep the conversation casual.

'Matthew's in the building trade,' Aunt Maud declared. 'Reconstruction.' Lucy would have plenty of questions to ask once they were alone, but in front of Aunt Maud she was showing no interest.

'And now he's doing odd-job gardening,' she said gaily. 'Talking of gardening, is that card from Joe?'

Aunt Maud's old gardener was at Eastbourne with his daughter, her husband and their children, and the card on the mantelpiece was scenes-of-Eastbourne. Aunt

Maud brought it down and Lucy read it to pass a few minutes.

Then Aunt Maud said, 'The gardens of Ivory Grange, where Lucy's Giles lives, are out of this world.' She went on to describe them as if she was taking Matt around the roses and through the water garden to the little folly of a pagoda on a hill overlooking the terrace and the pool.

He listened with suitable admiring murmurs until Lucy burst out, 'It's a nice garden. There are lots of nice gardens and I'm sure you're not particularly interested in this one.'

'Do they throw it open to the peasants?' he enquired gravely.

'Pity you missed last month for the local hospital,' she said. She stood up and replaced Joe's card, propping it carefully against an ebony elephant. 'I'll have to be going. Giles is in Manchester tonight; he's going to ring me.'

He might, although he had not said so. Matt got up as she did and suggested, 'Can I see you home?'

'Thank you.' If he had not offered she would have asked.

'Come and show me your ring,' said Aunt Maud. 'You get it tomorrow, don't you?'

'Yes I do, and I will,' Lucy promised. 'Now, could you spare a moment? I'd like to speak to you.'

'I'll be in the hall.' The little room was stocked like the Old Curiosity Shop, but Matt moved quickly through without disturbing a thing. Except me, thought Lucy. He had her so confused that she could have staggered. When he closed the door she said,

'I'm not happy about him staying here, even if it is only for a couple of nights. A stranger who just knocks on your door. For all you know he could be a right villain.' She added desperately, 'There are a lot of them about these days.'

'I'm sure there are.' Aunt Maud was unperturbed. 'But not Matthew. After I'd talked to him for a few minutes I knew that I should be quite safe and comfortable letting him stay. The vibrations, you know.'

'I get vibes, too,' said Lucy, 'and mine are giving out warning signals.'

'Now you're mocking,' said Aunt Maud. 'Matthew's all right, and a very knowledgeable young man, too.' She looked across at a glass-fronted corner cupboard, in which she had a collection of brownware pottery, none of it less than a hundred years old. 'When he saw my Dr Palmer he recognised it right away.' Three of the old gin bottles were crammed shoulder to shoulder facing outwards, crude models of Queen Victoria, John Wesley and Palmer-the-Poisoner, brown and shining like caramel and treacle toffee. 'He knows about Stafford-shire pottery,' said Aunt Maud.

Lucy bit her lip, undecided whether to say, 'He knows because I told him when I was telling him all about you and this house.'

Of course Aunt Maud felt he was no stranger, and maybe Lucy should explain why, but first she had to get him alone. She kissed Aunt Maud's leathery cheek, getting a pleased little start of surprise because although they adored each other Aunt Maud had never been the cuddly sort, and warned her, 'Don't sign anything until you see the colour of his money.'

He was at the front door. Lucy would not have been surprised to find him close enough to the parlour to be trying to eavesdrop. He was probably unscrupulous enough and the old doors were warped, but he would not have heard much if he had.

She set off fast up the road. There were still folk around and she wanted the scene to be quiet and deserted before she faced him. Striding beside her he said, 'You're in a hurry to get back for that phone call.'

'Yes.'

'Is the wedding date fixed yet?'

She and Giles had discussed it earlier in the week, when Giles had worked out when it would be easiest for him to take a break from the business and had come up with the middle of May. 'We thought May,' said Lucy who would have said 'No' if she had had her wits about her, because Matt said then,

'May's a good month for weddings, but you won't be going to Strona for the honeymoon.'

She gave a derisive 'Ha!'

'Where will you be going?' He sounded like an interested friend, and she kept a stony profile towards him as she strode on.

'Probably to see the Taj Mahal.'

'That's a tomb.'

'A very beautiful one. Would you mind shutting up until we get out of town? I live here. I know a lot of people. I don't want to create a scene and I think I might when we start talking. So please will you wait until I get home.'

'Are you asking me in?'

'I am not.' She walked on, fast and silently. She wanted to escape but this time she had nowhere to run and as they walked, never even brushing against each other, she was as conscious of him as though she was pressed against every inch of his body.

'How far?' he asked.

'Ten minutes at this rate. I'm sure you know the address. The Gables, Shady Lane.'

Under that picture he had read, 'Among the guests Lucinda Gillingham, daughter of solicitor Laurence Gillingham of Edgeford, Staffordshire, and Giles Lessing, son of Sir George and Lady Lessing.' Of course he knew her address, whether he had walked up to take a look at the place or not.

She said no more and neither did he as they left the little town and climbed the hill to reach Shady Lane, edging the heathlands of Cannock Chase. Once all the houses up here had been designed for prosperous and large families, but changing times had swept most of them away. The Gables, a handsome Victorian house in a large garden, was one of the few originals still standing.

As Lucy walked through the tall wrought-iron gates Matt said, 'Do I get to meet the rest of the family?'

'Not if I can help it.'

Her father and mother had been out when she came in from work and probably would not be back until late. The only lights, in one of the downstairs rooms, she had left burning, but she was not risking taking him into the house.

Night had fallen by now, the grass and the high yew hedges were silvered with moonlight and she led the way away from the half-circle drive and the three stone steps leading up to the front door, crossing the lawn to a stone bench set in an alcove of hedge.

She sat down and looked up at him. 'Well?' she said. 'Why did you come after me?'

'I wondered where you'd gone.'

There was a life-size statue beside the bench, both dating from the original landscaping of the gardens. A Grecian-style figure of a drapery-clad woman with— Lucy had always thought—a smile that seemed sinister with that blind white stare.

Matt was examining the statue while he was telling Lucy, 'Not enough to do much about it, although I did see the agent who lets the cottage. He said a relation of Miss Beale, the owner, had been there that week. Miss Beale was an eccentric old duck. He'd never seen her himself, she'd only been up once since she'd bought it, but he did have dealings with her.'

So he could have found her any time. She said, 'This happened as soon as I left.'

'Yes. Maud Beale was Great Aunt Maud, but you weren't Cindy Gill. You sounded as if you'd plucked that name out of thin air. You weren't telling anything about yourself, and you didn't hang around saying goodbye. That note sounded final enough, and as you know, I'm a man who can take no for an answer.'

Her cheeks burned in the darkness. He sat down beside her, but not touching her, stretching long legs and clasping hands behind his head, as if the stone seat was more comfortable than it was. He couldn't have been more relaxed.

'But,' he went on, 'would you believe it, in a dentist's waiting-room I opened a magazine and there you were smiling away. Great Aunt Maud Beale's wandering girl. I was in for a check-up and I got a clean bill, and I got up from that dentist's chair feeling pretty good. It was almost as though you'd brought me luck. I wanted to see you again. I wondered what you were up to these days. Just curiosity, you know.' He smiled the quick flashing smile that would have had her smiling back if she hadn't distrusted it. 'So I got an Edgeford directory and I looked up your father's address, then I looked up the Beales. There were three Ms and one for the Old Schoolhouse.'

He wouldn't need to ask the way; if he walked down the high street he'd find it. She said indignantly 'You don't want to buy the cottage.'

'I do. Straight up, it's a genuine offer. I've been looking around most of the summer. Besides, I've a weakness for eccentric old ducks; I've enjoyed meeting Maud. She told me all about you without my even having to ask. I just picked up that photograph of you in the silver frame and said, "What a beautiful girl".' He sighed deeply, but it was not heartfelt. He was still smiling, even if his smile was rueful. 'I came too late. You've got your future planned. Everything's working out for you.'

She believed it was a whim that had brought him here. Finding that cutting and deciding, for the hell of it, to look up 'Cindy Gill'. And there was no reason why his bid for the cottage should not be genuine. Aunt Maud who had only visited the place once since she had bought it, might well be open to offers.

Lucy hoped fervently that his offbeat humour would not tempt him into sticking around and rocking the boat for her.

'So how long are you staying?' she demanded.

'Not long.' A few days would be enough to do a lot of damage if he was that way inclined and she said worriedly,

'I should tell her you tracked her down through me, and that I told you all about her on Strona. An expert in Staffordshire pottery my foot, recognising Dr Palmer! He was another plausible devil.'

'Do you mind,' he said cheerfully, 'I hope you're not suggesting I'm in his league. They hanged him. And why didn't you tell her?'

He didn't need an answer to that and her voice was shrill and sharp with exasperation. 'Because I was supposed to be alone. I wouldn't even let Giles go with me; I said I had to be on my own.'

His drawl emphasised her edginess. 'We didn't plan to meet, and we hardly went around mugging the campers; it wasn't Bonnie and Clyde up there. No sex either. A blameless few days and the night we slept together you were swaddled up to your chin.'

He might laugh but she couldn't. Hearing him say 'the night we slept together' made her blood run cold. She made herself speak calmly. 'I've told nobody about you because there was nothing to tell, but if I have to say we met on Strona I will. It could be awkward for me and I'll see you don't get the cottage, but I would prefer you to keep your mouth shut. Will you?'

'But of course.' He sounded the most reasonable of men, her request granted as soon as asked. 'If you'd written on that note you left me, "Now I'm going home to the man I'm going to marry, goodbye and don't call me," I wouldn't have asked about you. And when I saw that magazine I'd have thought, good luck to you, Cindy-cum-Lucinda. And I wouldn't be here.'

She believed him. She hoped. Why should he cause trouble for her? She had done him no harm. And he looked and sounded sincere. After a moment she said, 'Can I say it now? I'm going home to the man I'm going to marry, goodbye and don't call me.'

'Good luck to you, Cindy-cum-Lucinda.' He moved fractionally closer, until there was hardly any distance between his face and hers and she seemed to be breathing the coolness of his skin. The headlights of a car came sweeping round the drive. It stopped in front of the house and a man and woman got out. Sylvia's long blonde hair and her silvery dress shimmered. She tossed back her hair and they heard her laughing. 'Who's that?' Matt asked.

'My mother.' At his start of surprise she said, 'As she tells everybody, she was a child bride.'

Sylvia had been twenty-two when she married, but in the moonlight she looked younger than Lucy. 'Your father?' said Matt.

'A very good friend of both of them,' said Lucy as the couple went into the house together. She stood up. 'Thank you for seeing me home. And, well, thank you.'

'You've nothing to thank me for,' he said, and she hoped that had no double meaning. Just now she was almost sure he had been going to kiss her—lightly enough, a goodbye kiss, but she would have been a fool to believe there was no danger in him. When he got up, unfolding himself from the bench, she realised again how tall he was.

'Goodnight,' he said and she watched him go, like a black panther she thought, across the grass and through the open gates; her breath escaped in a silent whistle of relief.

He had promised to keep his mouth shut, and she should be feeling safer for the first time since that cutting had fluttered on to her lap on Wednesday morning. In the moonlight the statue smiled its strange smile and Lucy shivered and clasped her arms tight around herself, touched by a sudden chilling conviction that there was nothing in the world to laugh at.

In the house the drawing-room door was open, light spilling into the hall, and as Lucy passed it her mother called, 'Hello. Everything all right?'

'Yes,' said Lucy, and she said hello to the man, a local farmer she had known all her life. He had a soft spot for Sylvia and had jumped at the chance of giving her a lift home from a party that she was finding tiresome.

'Jack gave me a lift,' her mother told Lucy. 'Your father was enjoying himself but I was getting one of my headaches.' She always looked fragile and appealing and Jack, ruddy-faced and weighing fifteen stone, said 'Poor little girl.'

Sylvia favoured him with a lingering smile and Lucy suggested, 'Coffee?'

He deserved something she supposed for bringing Sylvia home, although he probably considered the smile was ample reward. Lucy knew that Sylvia thought he was a bore, but admiring men were necessary to Sylvia Gillingham. She believed that their attentions kept her young, and something certainly did. Possibly the time and money she spent in beauty salons, health farms, and exclusive fashion stores.

Lucy quite liked Jack. When she took in the coffee tray he was chuckling at a spicy bit of gossip Sylvia was relating. She was laughing, too, and he wiped his eyes and said, 'Your mother's a caution.'

Lucy poured their coffee.

'What's all this about then?' Jack said. 'Our litle Lucy getting married.'

'I'm losing my baby,' said Sylvia, and now her smile was misty. 'It's hard to believe, but of course we couldn't be happier for them both. And Giles is the dearest of boys.'

At thirty-two, Giles Lessing was no boy, but he was the one they would have chosen out of all Lucy's admirers. Right from the first date when he arrived to collect her her father was always jovial and her mother flattered him and sent little messages to his mother.

Giles thought they were a smashing pair, loving Lucy as their only child as much as his parents, especially his mother, doted on him. They did love her, but she had always known in her heart that she could not rely on them. Even when she was a child Aunt Maud used to say, 'Take it with a pinch of salt,' when holidays or outings were planned together, because as often as not they ended up going their separate ways and neither of them taking Lucy. Or when they promised to turn up at schools for concerts and speech days. Even to be around for her birthday. But she had never lacked for material things.

Laurence Gillingham was head of the firm of solicitors, and when Lucy took a secretarial course after leaving school there had been some discussion whether she might move into his offices. But there had been no vacancy at the time and she had ended up on the local freebie.

She was a natural as a salesgirl—chatting up

customers, she usually managed to sell advertising space—and she wrote snippets of news and gossip for the editorial pages. She liked her work, she had friends and dates, and until she started going around with Giles she had thought she might well end up unmarried. Much better that than the kind of marriage her parents had. Aunt Maud was a spinster, still wearing the ring of a young man who had never seen his twenty-eighth birthday, and her life had been happy and busy. She showed no signs of being lonely.

But Lucy believed now that with Giles there was every hope of a true and lasting partnership. Last Saturday night she had come back with Giles and told her parents, 'Giles has asked me to marry him,' and she had never known them so proud of her. From then on she really was their darling daughter.

Now Jack Powell was teasing her. 'It seems no time since you were a skinny little kid.'

'I still am,' she said gaily, although her skinniness had long ago developed into long lovely legs and a tall slender strength, and the child's small, pointed face had a vivid beauty in the woman.

'I'll say this and I'll stand by it,' said Jack, as though he was facing hecklers. 'Young Giles Lessing might have had his pick of them but he chose the right one. You've done very well for yourself, my gal.'

Sylvia's smile vanished. Jack, as usual, was being a tactless oaf, emphasising that Giles had done the choosing, and she said with an acid sweetness that went right over Jack's head, 'It took Lucy quite a while to make up her mind; Giles isn't the only man who's wanted to marry her.'

Jack chuckled, winking at Lucy. 'Let him chase you until you caught him, eh?'

'You're a male chauvinist,' said Lucy. 'And next time you can make your own coffee. I'm off to bed; I need my beauty sleep. If I start going off I could lose him yet.'

Her mother made a snappish little sound of disapproval and Jack Powell laughed until his three chins wobbled as Lucy left them to their coffee and went out, closing the door behind her.

Of course everybody thought that Lucy was doing well for herself, marrying into the money that was Lessing Electronics, next in line for the small manor house and instantly elevated into the social standing of being the daughter-in-law of Sir Giles and Lady Lessing. Those were the reasons why her mother and father thought that Giles was 'the dearest of boys', but they were not Lucy's reasons for marrying him.

In spite of the two she had left in the drawing-room, out here in the hall the house seemed empty. The ticking of a grandfather clock was the only sound, and as she climbed the stairs she thought, not for the first time, that this house was much too big for a family of three that was about to be reduced to two. And that her father's complaints about its upkeep made sense.

Last month there had been a roof repair when some tiles had slipped and rain had started seeping in. 'This place is costing a fortune,' he had moaned. 'One of these days it will come tumbling down round our ears.'

Her mother had said, 'Why don't you sell it?' But there was no call any longer for houses like this, not even from property developers. There were still 'For Sale' notices outside new houses in Shady Lane and it was unlikely that anyone else would want to invest in another small local estate. 'Because you missed your chance, of course,' Sylvia had sneered. 'Typical.'

Now, as Lucy reached the top of the creaking staircase, shadows seemed to make patterns like cracks on the walls and she thought, it could fall down. Not because it's old but because nobody cares about it. It could come down like a house of cards because it's got no foundations. That was what she and Giles had. An understanding that had foundations on which they could build a future.

He did phone her. She was lying in bed, trying to read a book, when the phone rang and her mother called upstairs, 'Lucy, Giles.'

Sylvia was still in her silvery dress but she had kicked off her shoes and her hair looked mussed. Lucy could hear the televison and she asked 'Has Jack gone?' as she came down the stairs.

'Of course he's gone,' said Sylvia. 'I can't take more than five minutes of him. I wouldn't have given him coffee. Just a thank you and on your way. I'm watching an old movie.'

She looked like a star from an old movie herself. Lucy suggested, 'Why don't you go to bed if you've got a headache.'

'Headache? Oh, that. No, I'll see the film out.'

When her father came home there could be a slanging match, but Lucy would be in bed with the door shut, although she sighed as she sat down on the bottom of the stairs and cuddled the receiver and said, 'Hello, darling.'

'Just saying goodnight,' said Giles.

'Had a good day?'

'Fairish. Anything happened to you?'

She said 'No,' although Matthew Lomas coming back into her life was hardly a non-event. Giles would hear that somebody wanted to buy Aunt Maud's cottage but it wouldn't surprise him that Lucy had not mentioned it. It was a small cottage, a small business deal, and she could not start talking about it now, she would put it off until she saw him. She told him that Jack Powell had given her mother a lift home from a party, '... and he says that you must have had your pick of the girls because you're such a lovely fellow, but he thinks you chose the right one.'

Giles laughed. She could usually make him laugh; he said she brought out the sunshine. He said, 'Of course I did. Even old Jack's got enough sense to appreciate a good woman when he sees one.'

'It's my mother he thinks is the good woman,' she said gaily. 'He thinks I'm a skinny little kid, and my mother was sighing about losing her baby. Maybe you're cradle-snatching.'

She could hear herself talking rubbish and the murmur of Giles's laughter and his voice. Before he hung up he told her, 'I'll be around about seven. I've booked our table.'

'I'll be ready,' she said. 'Night, darling.'

'Dream of me.'

'I always do.' That was not true but it was what he wanted to hear. Tonight she hoped she would sleep without dreaming at all, but she was still awake when she heard her father's car and, a little later, banging doors. So they had had words before they went to their separate rooms.

She had never shared a room. From her cot she had been in this room, the nursery, where the bed had changed but not the furniture until Aunt Maud had come round with a delivery of pretty white and gold bedroom furniture she had just bought at an auction sale.

The room she shared with Giles would be in Ivory Grange and it would take some getting used to, sharing a room, a bed. When the words began blurring on the page Lucy put her book down, lay in the darkness, and tried to imagine Giles was beside her, that if she reached out she would touch him. She even mumbled, 'Goodnight, my darling,' and at last she slept.

She woke listening. Something had woken her, a muffled sound like movement in the room, and she groped blindly for the bedside lamp, staring around with wild dazzled eyes. Even when she knew the room was empty she was still breathing shallowly, her ears straining.

She could hear the wind; a window must have banged somewhere or a door. Nobody was coming up the stairs or standing just outside her room in the dark deserted corridor. But she could not rid herself of the feeling that Matt was near. It was imagination, her conscience troubling her. He was at Aunt Maud's sleeping soundly, not dreaming or thinking of her.

But in the end, after she had switched off the light, she had to get out of bed and go to the window. Pressed against the window frame she looked down into the gardens as if she might see him looking up at her. There were shadows down there, too, but none of them moved. He was not there. Perhaps a nightmare had woken her. something about Strona. And it was the time of night when problems loom largest. Matt was a problem that could disrupt her life, bringing it down like the house of cards. She tossed and turned. Her mind was buzzing until her head was aching and she knew that she never was going to get back to sleep.

She got out of bed again and went into the bathroom, opening the little wall cabinet and taking out the bottle of sleeping pills. They were prescribed for Sylvia who claimed to have spells of insomnia and liked a few to hand. Lucy never used them but tonight she tipped out one and swallowed it with half a glass of water. In the morning she would no longer be feeling desperate and trapped because of course she was not, but right now she needed to blank out. Which, as she was unaccustomed to tranquillisers, she promptly did.

She woke with a head that felt heavy but in the morning light everything was clear and uncomplicated. All that mattered was that Giles loved her and today he was going to put the ring on her finger that would show the whole world she was loved. It was going to be a wonderful day, and nothing and nobody was going to spoil it.

She heard the sound of her father's car starting up as she came out of the shower in the bathroom. He was off to meet Sir George in the clubhouse of the Beaudesert Golf Course and, from the blue skies she saw through her window, it would almost certainly keep fine for them.

Since Giles had decided he was serious about Lucy, Sir George and Laurence Gillingham had begun playing together regularly, but this would be their first game since Giles had actually asked Lucy to marry him. Both men were pleased about that. Both mothers, too. It was nice to be pleasing everybody. Even Aunt Maud's cards forecast health and happiness when she insisted on reading them for Giles a few weeks ago. She hadn't seen Matt in the cards. There had been no mention of a dark man. Reading Giles's fortune, she had come up with a clutch of hearts and diamonds and nothing at all to worry about.

Lucy went downstairs in a bright cotton dress, barelegged and sandalled. She was wearing no make-up and her hair was brushed loose. In the kitchen her mother was drinking coffee and reading the papers, her face discreetly prettied, lashes darkened, cheeks and lips brightened; Sylvia never emerged without her makeup. 'Nothing in the post,' she said as Lucy filled and switched on the kettle. 'You slept late didn't you?' She sounded accusing. Saturday was Lucy's day off but she was usually an early riser. 'I thought we might go shopping.' Her mother needed no excuse for spending money but she had one now. 'We ought to start on your trousseau. You haven't got much that will be suitable for when you're Giles's wife.'

'Oh, I don't know,' said Lucy. Sylvia was a label-snob; she only went for the exclusive names, while Lucy shopped around for what suited her and what she could afford. The few designer items in her wardrobe had all come from nearly new shops. She hadn't the cash for big spending and she was not asking her father to subsidise her. She would buy her trousseau when the wedding was nearer. 'Not today,' she said, and, before her mother could start arguing, 'Aunt Maud's had an offer for the cottage.'

Sylvia looked blank. 'The cottage? You mean her house?'

'The cottage on Strona. Somebody wants to buy it.'

'Oh, that,' said Sylvia. 'Good. Horrible little place.'

'She hasn't made up her mind yet. He's waiting for her answer.'

'Well, she'll have to read the tea leaves, won't she?' said Sylvia. 'I hope they don't tell her to give it away. I'll have another cup of coffee while you're making yours and then if you're not coming I'll be off.'

Housework kept Lucy busy all morning and in the afternoon she did a batch of baking. Betty, married and with teenage children, came in three days a week, but this house had been designed for a live-in staff and Lucy fought a never-ending battle to keep it clean and tidy.

After she had taken the last tray of small cakes out of the oven she shut the kitchen door and went upstairs. The rest of the time, until Giles called for her at seven, she was devoting entirely to herself. If anyone knocked on the door they could go away again. She was going to wash the dust out of her hair and the flour out of her fingernails and make herself lovely and silky and sensuous for tonight.

She bathed in her mother's bath oil, and gave her hair a beauty treatment with conditioner and hot towels. Lucy's hair was always healthy and shining but she was enjoying the cossetting. She painted her fingernails a

gold-flecked bronze that flattered her tan and spent a
long time fixing her face and her hair.

Giles liked her with her hair up and she pinned it
high, with tendrils falling over her smooth cheeks and
emphasising the bone structure of her face. Her dress
was a knock-out, too. An apricot chiffon, flattering and
fluid when she walked, cut low so that the antique gold
earrings and the matching collar Aunt Maud had given
her for her last birthday showed to advantage.

Last Saturday when Giles had asked her to marry
him, at the same restaurant and over the same table they
had booked for tonight, she had looked fine. She had put
in the usual effort before an evening out, and if she was
not the most attractive woman in the room she was a
close runner-up. But tonight she was going to be special
for him, and when she opened the front door and he saw
her it was all worthwhile.

'You look sensational,' he told her. She went into his
arms in the empty hall and thought how warm and safe
he made her feel.

'We could stay home,' she said. 'I could find a bottle,
although I can't promise it would be champagne.'

'I can,' he said. 'It's all waiting for us.' Giles was an
orderly man, he liked arrangements kept and he had
tonight planned. Last Saturday's dinner for two, in a
very expensive restaurant that had just opened, had
ended in coffee and brandy and Giles suddenly saying, 'I
think it's about time we got married.'

She had been expecting that. She hadn't known the
time or the place but she had known from all manner of
things that some day he would ask her to marry him, and
after hardly any hesitation she had said, 'I'd like that.'

He'd kissed her hand and said, 'I should have brought
a ring along.'

'Did you think I might say no?' she had teased, but he
had answered quite seriously,

'Of course I didn't. We'll do this again, next Saturday, and I will bring the ring.'

She had been asked during the week, 'Where's your ring?' and she had said, 'I get it on Saturday.' And when her friends wanted to know, 'What's it like?' she had told them to wait and see.

She was waiting to see herself and Giles was keeping it until the meal was nearly over. 'Have you got my ring?' she whispered when the waiter had taken their order and moved away. Giles smiled and nodded and patted his pocket.

'Can I see it?'

'All in good time.' He was kind and generous and he enjoyed little games like this. With inner amusement Lucy felt that she should lisp childishly, 'Pretty-please,' but she imagined Matt's sardonic laughter, and suddenly that joke would not have been funny.

She said, 'Aunt Maud's had an offer for the cottage on Strona.'

'A good one?'

'It seemed reasonable.'

'Is she selling?'

'She's thinking about it.' The wine waiter reached their table, showed Giles the label on the bottle, poured a little, and Giles went through the routine of tasting and approving. Lucy might have gone on to say, 'I met the man who wanted to buy when I was up there,' but this small disturbance had broken the continuity. She was not sure now that she could say that in the right offhand way; Giles was not particularly interested in Aunt Maud's old cottage.

He wanted to talk about their home, how his bachelor apartment in Ivory Grange could be enlarged for a married man. He had been giving it some thought, and Lucy listened and said it sounded wonderful.

Their table was shielded from the rest of the room by a

ceiling-to-floor trellis and some exotic climbing plants, almost like a private room. As Giles elaborated, 'We can make a guestroom out of one of the attics, knock down the wall at the end of the living-room and make a bigger kitchen,' she nodded, imagining it all.

It was good being with Giles, and in the home he was building for her there would be no angry voices, no arguments. She ate her meal of avocado soufflé followed by grilled Dover sole in a glow of contentment.

And when the coffee was poured, and the brandy glasses placed beside the cups, and Giles brought out the ring and set it on the table, his hand covering it, she must have looked as thrilled and bright-eyed as a birthday child.

'Show me,' she begged. He held the ring out to her, and she stared at the brilliant half hoop of five graduated diamonds. It was a family heirloom, of course, and Giles said, 'It was my great-grandmother's.'

'It is *beautiful*.'

He smiled, 'My mother says, you can't go wrong with diamonds.'

So it was coming with Lady Lessing's blessing and— as Lucy's mother had been saying ever since Giles started dating Lucy, again with his mother's blessing— Alys Lessing had exquisite taste.

Giles picked up her hand and put the ring on her finger. It stuck on the knuckle, needing slight pressure to get it on, and Lucy gasped, not just at the size of the diamonds, but because it was too tight. As she looked down her finger seemed to be puffing over it and Giles said, 'It doesn't fit, does it?'

It felt like a tourniquet and she had to admit 'No' as she tried to ease it off. Heaven knew how it had slipped on; there was no moving it back. She licked it and tugged but the ring remained firmly embedded, and all the time her finger was swelling.

Giles took her hand, looking as flushed as the finger, and she protested, 'I tell you I can't get it off and it's no good pulling.' He was hurting her and doing no good, and she had to bite down the giggles because he was really upset. He had meant this evening to be romantic and perfect and now in his eyes it was spoiled because the ring was the wrong size.

He babbled, 'I should have checked, my mother said was I sure it would fit and I said I was. You always seemed to have such tiny little hands.'

'About average.' Lucy felt a rush of sympathy and affection for him. 'But it's a beautiful ring and this doesn't matter; it can be fixed.' She wondered how long you had when the circulation was cut off before your finger went blue. Would the ring have to be damaged? An heirloom! Lady Lessing would not like that.

Her finger was throbbing and the ring wasn't shifting. A waiter coming round the trellis to offer a refill of coffee saw a lady in distress while her companion was tugging at her ring. He stood aghast, almost dropping the coffee-pot. 'Could we have some butter?' Lucy gasped.

'Ah, you want to get the ring off?' He backed away and she grinned.

'He thought you were taking it back. You'd brought me here to wine me and dine me and get your ring back.' But Giles was not amused. The waiter reappeared with several pats of butter and hovered sympathetically while Lucy greased her finger and tried to wriggle the ring off, and Giles looked hot and bothered.

They got it off at last, but it took time and it got the attention of more helpful members of the staff. A waitress brought a bowl of crushed ice which took down the swelling and when a final dab of butter slid the ring over the knuckle there was almost a restrained cheer.

The staff then retreated and Giles put the well-greased ring into a handkerchief and into his pocket. He couldn't get out of the restaurant fast enough. He hated scenes and whatever interpretation was put on what had just happened—whether it seemed like a lover's quarrel or whether they thought he had proposed with a ring the girl could never wear—he had looked a fool.

The restaurant was in another town. It was possible no one would recognise him, but he was sure the staff had been asked why there was all the fuss behind the trellis. He settled the account and made for the exit, deliberately avoiding looking anywhere else, and Lucy slipped her hand through his arm and squeezed and would have smiled if he had looked at her. 'I feel like a Cinderella who couldn't get into the slipper,' she said brightly.

'Yes,' said Giles.

Out of the corner of her eye she saw the table where a man sat alone. Matt raised a glass as she turned her head and she could have sworn his shoulders were shaking with silent laughter.

# CHAPTER FOUR

'DARLING,' said Lucy, 'so it didn't fit. That's no big deal; I can wait another few days.'

'If I was superstitious I'd say it was a bad omen,' said Giles morosely. 'Your Aunt Maud would.'

'That is nonsense.'

They were in his car, driving towards Lucy's home, and Giles was still convinced that the waiters and probably half the diners had been laughing behind his back.

Lucy had been laughing, too. When the ring came off she had given a hoot of triumph and he was sure she was suppressing giggles until they got outside the restaurant.

She was serious now. At some traffic lights when he turned towards her he saw the shadow on her face and said mournfully, 'It spoiled our evening.'

'That's another nonsense.' She leaned back in her seat, her head thrown back and her eyes closed as if weariness had suddenly claimed her. 'As hitches go,' she said, 'believe me, that was nothing.'

Her voice was harsher than he had ever heard it and for a moment she seemed unreachable. Then the lights changed, behind them a car hooted and they moved on, and after a while he said, 'You're right, of course but you're disappointed. I promise you'll have your ring in no time at all. The right size this time.'

But it was not disappointment she was holding in check, it was anger. Matt had followed her to that restaurant tonight. Aunt Maud knew where they were going and she must have told him. What had she expected him to do, stroll up and introduce himself and join the party? As soon as Lucy could get to a telephone the lines to Aunt Maud's would be scorching.

With her hair colour she was often asked if she had a temper and she could always smile and shake her head because she didn't think she had. She hated rows; she heard enough of them at home. She avoided arguments whenever she could, but since Matthew Lomas had reappeared she had discovered that she could be very angry and very raucous.

She had almost marched over to his table in that restaurant and told him what she thought of him. She would do that, but not with Giles beside her. Giles had been mortified by a silly little thing like a ring getting stuck on her finger, and if he had to learn about Matt a slanging match in a crowded restaurant would be no way to tell him.

'What?' she said, because Giles was talking to her, and he repeated.

'That ring, does it fit your left hand?' The only ring she was wearing was the keeper. She pulled it off her right hand and slipped it on to her engagement finger. 'Put it in my pocket,' he said.

Perhaps she should warn him not to be in too much hurry to get the diamond hoop changed because she might not be wearing it after all. When she came back from Strona she should have said, 'There were people around. I met some.' Then, when Matt came, she could have said, 'Yes, I met him.'

But she had said nothing and Giles would only have to look at him to know why. He had the physical impact of good looks, and an athlete's body, but so had other men. What set him apart was the excitement he generated. Mornings on Strona she had waited for him to arrive as though the day couldn't start until he did, and when he came it had been like an electric charge in the air. Maybe it was energy. Or devilment. But Giles would dislike and distrust Matthew Lomas and from there he would surely come to distrust Lucy.

When they reached her home he said goodnight. It was lateish and he was seeing her in the morning when the photographer was due at the Gables to take their photographs for the 'Our Bride of the Year' picture in Lucy's paper. If she had coaxed him into the house he might have changed his mind but she said, 'All right,' and brushed his cheek with cool lips.

She stood on the steps watching him drive away. Last night it had been Matt disappearing through the gates, after he had promised her it was goodbye. Some goodbye when he was spying on her tonight! She looked down at her strappy gold sandals and considered walking down to Aunt Maud's, then telling her the facts and waiting for Mr Lomas. Only it was too late and she was not dressed for walking alone through the night. But if she could slip into the house and through into the garage she could drive down. The front door opened as she put her key in the lock and her mother called, 'Come in. We've been waiting for you.' She peered past Lucy. 'Where's Giles? We heard the car.'

'Didn't you hear it drive away again?'

'Oh.' Sylvia pouted. She was wearing a peppermint green suit that Lucy had not seen before so her day had not been wasted, and Lucy's father was smiling as they reached the open door of the drawing-room. Then he too, asked 'Where's Giles?'

'He went home,' said Lucy.

'Everything all right?' There was concern in his voice although he had never worried about her until Giles Lessing had wanted her.

She said, 'Yes.'

'Show us the ring,' her mother said gaily, coming round from behind Lucy and looking down at the bare hand. Her own hand flew to her face, and she stared through splayed fingers. 'You don't have a ring.'

'It didn't fit,' Lucy explained. 'He thought I had a dainty little hand like his great-grandmother but I didn't.' Sylvia pealed with girlish laughter.

'You know what I thought? I thought he'd changed his mind. I'm a ninny. Well, tell us what it's like.'

Her face was bright with anticipation as she curled up like a kitten on the sofa, and Laurence relaxed in the dark red leather armchair that was his favourite seat.

Nobody Lucy knew had parents who looked as good as hers; this could have been a scene of happy family life in a TV movie. For the moment the warmth and the affection were real. They were happy together and proud of her and she wished it could always be like this. She sat down on the rest of the sofa and described the ring.

'Five big diamonds, but it was a little ring, and it got stuck on my finger, which started swelling. We needed a dish of butter and a bowl of crushed ice to get it off. Now he's taken the keeper ring to get the right size.'

They were both smiling but when she said, 'Giles didn't think it was funny. It did create rather a scene,' they both looked serious.

'Giles is a very sensitive young man,' Sylvia said hastily, 'and I'm sure you didn't make a fuss.'

'No more than I had to to get the ring off,' said Lucy. 'My finger was turning blue.'

'Yes, well . . .' Sylvia gestured vaguely as though it would have been better for Lucy to suffer in silence and never mind about the agony rather than embarrass Giles. Then she cheered up and beamed at Laurence and urged, 'Now tell her about your day.'

The last Lucy knew he had been off to play golf with Sir George and he was looking very self-satisfied. 'Did you have a good game?' she asked. 'Did you win?'

'Old George did; I'm no fool.' Laurence chuckled. He was the better player; perhaps he had let Sir George win. 'We were talking business,' he said. He had a glass containing a little whisky on a small table beside his chair. Now he raised the glass and sipped as though he was toasting something and announced, 'George is thinking of buying the house.'

'This house?' Lucy gasped. 'What for?'

'Who cares what for?' trilled Sylvia.

'They'll knock it down, of course,' said Laurence. 'Or let it fall down, but I don't mind telling you that the price we were discussing will make a lot of difference to our future.' He drank the rest of the whisky like the cat with the cream.

Lucy asked in a husky little voice, 'Is he only interested in the house because Giles is marrying me?'

Her father thought that was obvious. 'Well, he wouldn't be buying it on the open market. It might be passed off as a tax loss but it's hardly a viable business prospect. He's taking it off our hands because we're family now.' He beamed fondly at her. 'It was the best day's work you ever did when you brought Giles Lessing home.'

'And *I* don't mind telling you,' Sylvia said, looking hard at her husband and then around the big high-ceilinged room, 'that I don't know whether I could have stood another winter here, or whether I'd have been off to somewhere warmer.'

There was a threat there, although she said it gaily. The drain on resources from this old house could have parted them in the end. 'I can't get out of here fast enough,' said Sylvia as though there were bars on the window, and she uncurled herself and went over to Laurence and planted a kiss on the top of his head. 'Suddenly everything's working out,' she said.

That was what Matt had said last night—'You've got your future planned; everything's working out for you'—but more than Lucy's own happiness was at stake now. The sale of the house was good news. Tomorrow she would tell Giles how pleased she was about it. He hadn't mentioned it but she presumed he knew that his father had been going to bring up the matter with her father that morning.

'And your father thinks Aunt Maud should sell the cottage,' said her mother. 'She's never had an offer before and she's lucky to get this one.'

'Like us,' said Lucy. She yawned and stood up. 'The offers are pouring in and I'm off to bed.'

They followed her, she heard them come up, but she undressed and washed and gave them time to settle for the night before she put on her dressing-gown and went down again. Matt should be back by now even if he had stayed until the restaurant closed.

Aunt Maud's phone was in her kitchen. She might be in there mixing one of her hot milk nightcaps with whatever flavour she fancied tonight. That varied from a pinch of salt to a slug of whisky. But it was Matt who answered and Lucy kept her voice low, although the lights were out on the landing and the bedroom doors were closed. She asked, 'Is Aunt Maud there?'

'She's gone to bed. Have you ever had nutmeg in hot milk? She's left me a mug of it and it's not a flavour I can recommend.'

She ignored that and said briskly, 'She'll have to wait then. You'll do for now. Why were you at Boulders tonight?'

'For a meal.'

'Now that's what I call a coincidence. Fifteen miles away and you just wander in? And how did you get a table? I'm sure they're booked up on Saturday nights.'

'A cancellation,' he said. 'I was lucky.' None of this mattered; she was wasting time.

'Why did she let you do it?' she snapped.

'Hold on. Maud didn't send me;' she didn't know I was there. I asked her about the places around and she mentioned Boulders, where Giles proposed to you last week and you were going this evening. She said they specialised in seafood, which is a weakness of mine.' She knew he was grinning, 'Pity about the ring.'

'How do you know about that? Who told you?'

'Didn't you notice the hush?'

'What hush?'

'You've got a very carrying voice. When you screeched, "I tell you I can't get it off and it's no good pulling," that stopped most of the table talk. After that most of them were more interested in what was going on behind the screen. And when the butter and ice were rushed in——'

'I don't believe a word of this.' But he must have heard what she said and the rest of the action would have sounded hilarious, interspersed with her gasps and cries. If Giles knew he would be highly indignant, but she wanted to laugh so badly that she nearly put down the phone, because she was doing no laughing with Matt.

'Fine upstanding young man, your Giles,' he said. 'I wanted to see him.'

'You wanted to embarrass me.'

'I wouldn't have come up to you. I wouldn't even have acknowledged you. Although he did look like a man who embarrasses easily, and not much sense of humour either.'

She found herself saying stupidly, 'He does have a

sense of humour. He can be very funny.'

'Not the same thing,' said Matt.

She made a belated attempt to keep this conversation short and sharp. 'I'm not standing here discussing Giles with you. Just stay out of my way. Just keep right away from me.'

'Right,' he said, and she put down the phone. Tomorrow she would tell Giles about Matt, emphasising that their meeting on Strona had been brief and impersonal. Nobody could prove anything else, but until she called Matt's bluff she was wide open to blackmail.

She went downstairs next morning to find her mother and father already drinking coffee together in the kitchen, not a thing they often did, and discussing where they would go when the house was sold—they had to stay local, because of Laurence's business. Sylvia looked younger than ever in a pale blue silk dress, her eyes shining, brimming over with enthusiasm. Laurence, casual in sports gear—it was squash at the club this morning—also seemed to have shed years. The house had been a burden on his shoulders and now it was lifting.

'Hello, poppet,' he greeted Lucy. 'Sleep well?'

She said yes, although she had had better nights.

'We're looking through the property pages,' said her mother. A Sunday paper was open on the table. 'But there doesn't seem to be anything round here. I'll get in touch with some estate agents tomorrow.'

'Don't you think we should wait until we're sure this house is sold?' Lucy ventured and got protests from both of them. Laurence knew what old George had said and that was good enough for him. Sylvia could not bear to waste a minute.

'We've got to know where we're going and there's so much to be done. Not only that, but the wedding's in May. There are all the preparations for that. The time will fly, it will simply rush by.'

Lucy heard her mother's voice getting higher and the clock ticking on the kitchen wall, and suddenly it seemed to her that the words and ticking quickened, faster and faster, into a single high-pitched note. She had the oddest sensation, as if she was on a roller-coaster or a runaway horse, something that was rushing her willy nilly into god-knew what. And she heard her name called.

'*Lucy!*' It was her mother, or maybe her father, and the sensation ebbed and the clock ticked its separate seconds. 'Are you all right?' asked Sylvia.

'Yes.'

'Of course she's all right,' said Laurence. He drained his coffee cup, picked up his *Sunday Times* and said he would see them later. Sylvia reached across the table to touch Lucy's hand.

'You're cold,' she said, her voice rising again this time in surprise.

It was surprising because the morning was warm and the room was warm. Lucy managed a small smile. 'Over-excitement, I guess.'

'Could be a summer chill.' Sylvia leaned even further forward, mouthing rather than speaking aloud, 'You're not pregnant?'

'No, I am not.'

'Giles's mother would have a fit if you were and we don't want her turned against you.'

'Don't worry,' Lucy said wearily.

Her mother, looking relieved, hastened to add, 'Giles is a lovely man but—well, he does have rather a mother-fixation. Still, if it's only wedding nerves you've no problems.'

You think not, thought Lucy. She said, 'The photographer's coming at ten.'

'And brides-to-be are supposed to look radiant,' said Sylvia, because there were shadows under Lucy's eyes and it would be awful if she was catching something. Odd viruses were always around and this was no time for Lucy to be falling sick.

Sylvia had immediately discounted her panic that her daughter could be pregnant. The girl had too much common sense and Giles was hardly the passionate type who might have swept her off her feet. Maybe the fuss and the excitement were telling on her but it would be worse than a nuisance if stress affected her looks. Sylvia thought beauty was all-important in a woman and Giles Lessing had not married Lucy yet.

Fred the photographer arrived a few minutes before Giles. A lanky, balding young man, he wanted to get this job over with—he and his wife had other plans for their Sunday—but before he had time to become impatient Giles's Daimler was turning into the drive.

Sylvia and Laurence greeted Giles as if he was a dear friend they hadn't seen for ages, and he kissed Lucy and told her she was looking lovely.

'Come on, lovebirds,' said Fred. 'Let's get this show on the road.'

Giles looked askance and Lucy reminded him, 'This is Fred Owen. He's come to take our picture for the *Herald*.'

'Yes, of course.'

Giles was not photogenic with his pleasant blunt features but he had agreed, and he let Fred take over with a fairly good grace. They were photographed sitting side by side on the sofa—'Just look into each other's eyes.' And outside under the cedar tree—'Put your arm round her. That's right. Give her a kiss then.'

Giles did not, but he did look at Lucy with deep affection and she thought how dear he was and how much she loved him, and tried with all her heart to show that when she looked at him.

'That should do it,' said Fred, with what he considered a good selection in the bag. He winked at Lucy and patted her cheek and told Giles, 'You're a lucky guy, she's a cracker. I've always fancied her something rotten.'

'Now he tells me.' Lucy laughed, but when Fred drove away Giles said,

'He's very familiar.'

'He was joking,' she protested.

'I didn't like it.' She almost said, 'Oh, don't be so stuffy, he's mad about his wife,' but Giles went on huffily, 'You belong to me now and I don't like other men leering at you.'

'We're workmates,' said Lucy.

'Not for much longer,' Giles said.

Sylvia said quickly, 'Isn't it marvellous about the house? You do know about the house?'

Giles did, and he also knew of a superb apartment, attractively located, that they could get at a very low price. Lucy thought, I do belong to him and I can understand that he would object to me having any dealings with the likes of Matt. But it also seems that I can't even take a gentle ribbing from the likes of Fred.

She might have been on the defensive today because her conscience was raw, but it seemed that Giles was becoming even more possessive. He was cheerful and complimentary and in good spirits but Lucy felt that he kept a tightening hold on her. His hand was either on her arm or round her shoulders and she wished she could stop thinking that that was all it was, a light pressure, nothing like the shock of sensation that Matt's touch released in her.

She was lunching at Giles's home. Her mother was

lunching out, too, and her father was off to his club, and they all parted with smiles and friendly words. In the car Giles turned on music, the sun was shining and everything was almost too good to be true, and she wondered again and again if she would do better to let things ride. Open confession might be good for the soul but she doubted if it would do her relationship with Giles much good. In the meantime the sun shone in a bright blue sky and Giles was humming more or less in tune with the music, and when they reached Ivory Grange the front doors were open as though everyone beyond those doors was waiting for them.

The house was white stone four-storey Georgian, the most desirable residence for miles around, just as Sir George and Lady Lessing were the cream of local society. As Giles and Lucy walked into the hall, Alys Lessing came forward to envelop Lucy in a scented embrace.

Alys never failed to live up to her position. With her silver hair, always smoothly and beautifully styled, her couture clothes and her honest belief that she and her menfolk were a cut above almost everyone, she was a natural for lady of the manor. She had decided, about the same time as Giles, that Lucy Gillingham might be the girl for him. There had been other girls, of course, but Giles did not realise how much he had been influenced, for his own good, into cooling those relationships. Lucy was a sweet girl, pretty, helpful, bright, and it was time that Giles was settling down.

His mother stood back, smiling and gracious. 'And what a very charming dress. But then, you always look charming.'

'Thank you,' said Lucy.

'What a pity about the ring. But you'll have it very soon and next Sunday we'll have one of our little parties, a little celebration.'

During this hot summer there had been several lunch parties here, with a buffet set out in the orangery, and guests lounging around the pool, sunbathing and swimming. Friends, business contacts, employees and local celebrities had mingled and Lucy had helped as Giles's girlfriend, moving around, seeing that plates and glasses were filled. But on Sunday she would be wearing his ring, one of the family now and no longer in the background.

'You invite who you like,' said Alys. 'We'll make up a list,' she went on, 'only don't let Maud start telling fortunes.'

That was a little joke. Maud Beale was too bizarre for Alys Lessing's taste, but she was a good-hearted soul and a little eccentricity in the elderly could always be laughed off. Maud had not been the problem when Alys realised her son could become serious about Lucy Gillingham.

Now she said, 'Run along, dear. You'll find your father somewhere around. Lucy and I want a moment to ourselves.'

Do we? thought Lucy, and watched Giles walk away with wry amusement. Sir George and his son ran a thriving business, but away from the works Alys Lessing was boss. She treated both of them as if they were small boys, but she was caring and Lucy found it rather endearing.

Now she was walking upstairs and Lucy dutifully followed. She knew the house fairly well, Giles's apartment best of all, but this was the first time she had been into the master bedroom. From the deep pile of the white carpet to the rich patina of furniture and fittings, everywhere spelled wealth and luxury. Lucy could easily have found herself staring around, which would probably have been considered ill-mannered. The first time Giles had brought her home she had said, 'What a perfectly splendid house,' and Lady Lessing had said, 'Oh, yes,' in chilly tones as if she thought Lucy was coveting it.

Since then Lucy had avoided overpraising anything. What she had been brought in here to see was lying on the bed, folded in leaves of yellowing tissue paper. Alys asked, quite anxiously, 'Do you have a family veil?'

So this was another heirloom, like the ring of flashing diamonds. 'No,' said Lucy. Her mother had married in a stylish gown and hat. In wedding photographs Lucy's parents had looked stunning as film stars, but there was no thought of putting anything aside for a future daughter to wear at her wedding.

'Then you must wear this,' said Alys. 'You'll be the fourth generation.' She raised it reverently from its wrappings. It was a beautiful veil, embroidered with lovers' knots and flowers in tiny seed pearls, cream-coloured now rather than white, and well preserved although it had to be fragile as gossamer.

Alys was handling it carefully but Lucy gasped, 'How awful if it fell apart.'

'It will stand one more wearing and then perhaps we can have it made up into a christening robe.'

Lucy stood mute; she dared not think that far ahead.

'Come and see.' Alys indicated a cheval mirror and Lucy crossed to it. Alys draped the veil over Lucy's head and shoulders and Lucy held it in place with fingertips. She was almost afraid to touch it in case it disintegrated. 'I've been saving it for Giles's bride, of course,' said Alys, talking to the reflection, 'and I'm so glad it's you.'

Lucy looked at the face of the girl in the mirror and wondered why Lady Lessing could not see worry there, smiling a forced smile.

But Giles's mother's smile was happy enough. 'I don't mind telling you, my dear, that I don't have much time for modern girls.'

'I'm a modern girl.'

'Of course you are, but you're not one of the wild ones.' She laughed at the very idea of Lucy running wild, and Lucy took off the veil that smelled of cedarwood and had to be stored in the open cedarwood chest at the foot of the bed. 'Please take it,' she begged. 'It's so beautiful and so delicate.'

'You'll be a beautiful bride.' Lady Lessing began to fold and rewrap the billowing cloud. 'And something else I don't mind telling you now and this will be our little secret. I did have some doubts at first. I know I'm old-fashioned but I've always had a horror of scandal. Giles takes after me in that, and—forgive me but, well, there's always talk in a small town about anyone who——'

'Aunt Maud?' Lucy burst out laughing. 'Oh, I've never heard of Aunt Maud causing a *scandal*. I admit she does make herself felt on all those committees and since the murals on the schoolroom walls the vicar hasn't been too keen on holding the jumble sales in there.'

She was talking rubbish but suddenly Alys Lessing, cocooned in wealth and respectability, seemed incredibly stupid.

'Oh, no,' said Alys. 'Not Maud. Your mother.' Lucy's lips set and Alys said placatingly, 'She is such an attractive woman, looks so young. She always has.' She touched her own lacquered hair and Lucy thought, you're jealous. 'But she does have rather a flirtatious manner and at first I wondered if you were—well, as lively and as popular as she is. Of course, as I got to know you better I knew that you would take your marriage vows as seriously as I do myself, and that my son's happiness would be safe with you.'

She got up stiffly from replacing the veil in the chest and let the lid drop with a little bang. Lucy would have given anything to be able to say that her mother was worth a dozen of her, and perhaps Sylvia Gillingham was. But she was popular and lively and by that Lady Lessing meant that she was outrageously attractive and imprudent.

Lucy knew instinctively that Giles's mother had investigated her. Discreetly of course, talking with friends, making casual enquiries, but all she would have learned was that Lucy had had boyfriends but none that amounted to much and never a breath of scandal. So she could wear the heirlooms, the ring and the veil. Lady Lessing was acting as if she had paid her a compliment.

'My goodness,' she said quite merrily, 'the men will be wondering what's happened to us and we have other guests for lunch, too, and here we are having our litle chat. I do wish the ring had been the right size. There are others, of course, but Giles chose that one and I'm sure he knows what your taste is. Oh, you're very right for each other, my dear.'

Lucy wondered if this had also been a warning about what was expected of her in the future. She liked Giles's mother. She had envied him that single-minded devotion and very soon she had learned that Alys approved of her. Giles had told her, 'My mother likes you,' quite early on. Everybody knew that Sylvia Gillingham had a racy reputation, and it was understandable that Alys might be concerned, but it was tactless to mention it. These last few days Lucy had found her tolerance threshold slipping.

She walked downstairs, listening to Alys. In this house it was usually Alys Lessing doing the talking. Now she was saying, 'Our other guests are Robert and Marion

Brownlow, the Dean of Wichfield Cathedral and his wife. The wedding will be in the cathedral on the fourteenth of May.'

Lucy knew that the Brownlows were coming to lunch and she knew the date of the wedding, but she was beginning to resent Alys Lessing's assumption that everything would be done her way. She was beginning to see Giles's mother as complacent and prejudiced and stupid.

The Dean and his wife were none of those things, and they congratulated Giles and Lucy warmly. They were a good advertisement for marriage, having just had their ruby wedding and looking so well on it.

'May's a lovely month,' said Marion Brownlow, a handsome horse-faced woman with a warm and charming smile.

'It's the best time for Giles to take a holiday from work,' said Alys.

Lucy imagined the effect if she said, 'May could be an unlucky month for me. Last May I got married on Strona and that hasn't done me much good.'

Across the table at Ivory Grange everybody was in good humour and good form. Good food was served, the talk flowed easily and nobody saw anything wrong in Lucy. She answered brightly when she was spoken to, and nobody noticed that the rest of the time she was quiet.

Windows overlooked impeccably tended gardens and Lucy was seated so that she only had to raise her head to look out. She found herself studying shadows, her eyes caught by the slightest movement when a bird flew low or a breeze stirred the leaves of a tree. She knew that Matt would not be out there, but she felt his presence and it scared her so that she hardly tasted the food she was swallowing.

What it really came to was that she couldn't stop
thinking about him. She was here, with her new family
and friends, and all the time she was looking for Matt.
She looked at the Brownlows and they were nice, they
really were. Then she looked at Sir George and Alys and
Giles and they were nice, too. She was going to spend the
rest of her life with Giles, and if she did tell him that she
had met Matt before the worst thing she could do was
add, 'And since he tracked me down I haven't been able
to get him out of my mind, day or night.'

After lunch they sat out on the terrace and after a
while Giles and Lucy wandered off, around the gardens.
Behind the first hedge he kissed her and she kissed him
back. Then she asked him, 'How do you love me?'
Through her mind went Elizabeth Browning's lines for
her Robert: 'How do I love thee? Let me count the ways.
I love thee to the depth and breadth and height my soul
can reach.'

'How?' Giles thought it was the wrong word. The
question surely was why? 'Because you're very beautiful,' he said, 'and very sweet.' She looked at him, her
eyes still questioning. 'And we're very happy together
and we'll have a good marriage.'

He stroked her hair and ran his hands down her
shoulders and back, pressing her closer to him, and she
wondered if soaring ecstasy could grow from this
comforting closeness so that nothing else in the world
would matter. She asked, 'How do you feel when I kiss
you?'

'Good.'

'I don't set fire to your blood?'

'That sounds rather uncomfortable.' He was smiling
at her and there was none of the power that could have
drawn her and Matt together like two planets on a
collision course. She wished he would lose control for a

moment, but Giles would have died of shame at being caught in any state of real intimacy, and somebody else could come strolling round that hedge.

He said, 'Mother showed you the veil.'

'It's beautiful, but very fragile.' They walked on through the rose garden, holding hands. 'We had a little chat,' she told him. He raised an eyebrow at that. 'She said she wasn't sure about me at first.' That made him smile again.

'Not for long.'

'If I had had a past I'd have been out of the running?' She smiled as she said it.

'Mother's old-fashioned,' said Giles.

'So she said.'

He defended her hastily, 'On the whole her standards are the right ones. She's always given me good advice. Her reasons for loving you are some of the reasons why I do. She's an idealist and so am I.'

He turned her towards him, speaking gravely and tenderly. 'I love you because I can trust you. I know you'd never lie to me, or cheat on me. You're good.' Then he smiled again. 'As well as being so beautiful. Mother was right. You're the one I was waiting for.'

She got away late afternoon when the Dean and his wife had to leave. They were passing the end of her road and she said, 'I must be going soon, too. I've got some work to finish tonight. An article I have to hand in in the morning.'

Giles said that of course he would run her back, but there wasn't much point in both cars covering the same ground. Lucy kissed all the Lessings and as they walked towards the Dean's car Giles asked, 'Are you all right?'

'A bit of a headache.'

'Too much sun. You should wear a hat.'

The afternoon had seemed very long. She couldn't

relax; she needed to get away. When the Brownlows dropped her at her gate she waved, smiling, and then walked slowly towards the house.

It was empty. There was no answer when she called, 'Anyone in?' from the hall, and she went up to her room and flopped down on the bed. Staring at the ceiling didn't help but one thing was clear. The sooner Aunt Maud made up her mind about the cottage and Matthew Lomas left town, the better. If he and Giles ever met she was on a slippery slope.

She went down again into the hall and dialled Aunt Maud's number. 'Hello?' said Maud Beale, who always answered the phone as if she expected to hear something interesting.

'It's Lucy. Have you decided about the cottage yet?'
'I think I shall let him have it.'
'I think so, too,' said Lucy. 'When will he be leaving?'
'Would you like to talk to him? He's here.'
'No, thank you.' She was sure Aunt Maud was waving her phone in Matt's direction. She put her own phone down and when it rang almost immediately she ignored it. If the sale was settled he had no excuse for hanging around and she did not want to talk to him. She had nothing to say that she had not said already.

She made herself a cup of instant coffee and went outside, where the sun was still shining, to sit in the shade of the cedar tree and drink it. It was a big garden. Once there had been garden parties held here, croquet matches played on the lawn. There was still a tennis court but old Joe was gardener here, too, and by the time he got back from his holidays the grass was going to be too much for him. They would have to get somebody in to cut it although, sitting here, drinking her coffee, Lucy supposed she should be trying to get the lawnmower going herself.

She wasn't keen. It was a brute of a machine; only Joe seemed to have the knack. But she wheeled it out of the shed, turned the 'on' switch and began to yank the pullcord. Half a dozen jolting jerks hardly raised a splutter and when the engine did finally catch it chugged the length of the lawn and turned on her when she tried to get it round to come back. Well, that was how it felt. Somehow her hand was wrenched and one of her fingernails was bent back. She let go with a howl of pain.

The engine stalled and stopped and she surveyed her split nail. On her ring hand, too, the hand that would be on display any time now, so that took care of the next fifteen minutes; she would be doing a repair job. She sat at her dressing-table, gluing and patching, and then she repainted the gold-flecked varnish to hide the flaw. At the end it looked fine, so long as she remembered it was brittle.

When the varnish was dry she put on a thick pair of gardening gloves and went out to have another go at the wretched mower. It should have been replaced years ago. She started off again, jerking the pull cord, getting a punishing kickback but no spark until she was gasping for breath. When the cord whipped out of her hand, sending her off-balance, she snarled, 'Start, you perisher,' and, still sprawling, kicked it.

'So you're the girl who beats up lawnmowers,' said Matt. 'You've flooded the carburettor.'

'I don't know about flood it, I'd like to drown it.' She propped herself up on an elbow, cupping her chin in her hand. 'I suppose you fell out of the trees. And don't say Aunt Maud sent you.'

'All right, I won't.'

'Did she?'

'She said you wanted to know when I'll be leaving.'

'Well?'

'Is that what you want?'

Of course it was. She spoke slowly, deliberately, with a slight pause between each word for emphasis. 'I—want—you——' But when he started to grin she finished hastily, 'to shove off.' He went on grinning.

'Shall I look at your lawnmower first?'

She would like to see it knock him flat. 'How kind,' she said.

'Give it a minute.' He sat down beside her on the grass, and she nibbled her jagged nail—it had broken, of course—and asked 'When are you going?'

'I'm painting the schoolroom for her first.'

Not before time, but it was not what Lucy wanted to hear. She sighed deeply and a silence settled that was not bothering him. He looked very comfortable, and when he did get up he did it reluctantly.

As he switched on the mower she said, 'Don't blame me if it kicks you in the teeth.'

'Of course I shall blame you; you kicked it first. Come on, mate, do your best for me and I'll keep her off you.' He was stronger than she was, yanking the cord, he gave it a firmer steadier pull, and he was not going to tire either, although it seemed to catch maddeningly quickly and idled healthily while he stripped off his shirt and tossed it on to the grass.

Now it was a pussy cat, positively purring, making lovely long straight lines, better than Joe had managed for years. Lucy watched him as he went to and fro with that easy animal grace and thought, I know your body better than I know Giles's. I know how brown and strong it is and how the muscles move. I don't know your mind right now, but I could fool myself that I do, and that that was why I came back here, because you were coming.

She had no busines lolling around feeling relaxed and contented and she was about to get up when the mower stopped. That was a pity, with the back lawn almost finished. She said, 'I told you it was temperamental.'

'It's out of petrol. Have you got any?'

'I don't think so.'

'That's it then.' He sat down again and said 'She showed me her photograph album this morning. You as a child.'

Like the doting grandmother. Lucy grimaced. 'That must have been very boring for you. I remember some of them.'

'There was one of you lined up after a school play. A sad little face, trying to smile because your parents hadn't turned up and you were the star of the show.'

She could imagine Aunt Maud leafing through the album, becoming sentimental and confiding. God knew, Lucy's childhood was none of Matt's business and she said, 'I don't remember that,' although she did, vividly.

He went on. 'She said, "I only hope Lucy isn't marrying for security".'

It was too bad of Aunt Maud to discuss her like this with a stranger, and anyhow security was not a bad thing. She said coldly, 'Where on earth did she get that idea?'

'She said that Giles is reliable, and your parents aren't.'

It shocked her that Aunt Maud had told him she had ever been neglected. Nobody else said that and it was a long time since it mattered; at twenty-three she was capable of looking after herself. She said, 'Aunt Maud was always fanciful and she's getting worse. Giles and I are getting married because we love each other.' His eyes gleamed with something that could have been laughter or scorn, or even anger.

'Not because the Lessings are loaded?' he said softly, and it happened again, the urge to hit him so that her open hand almost took a swipe at him. She looked at it in mid-swing as though it belonged to somebody else, and jerked it down. 'Why did you run out on me in Strona?' he asked. 'Why didn't you stay to say goodbye?'

'Because it was easier just to go.'

'Do you always take the easy way out?'

Why not, if there was an easy way? But she couldn't look him in the face because she knew that he would consider compromise a kind of cowardice. 'Not always,' she said.

'But you're not telling Giles that we've met before?'

'Maybe I should? I think you will. As you said, it was nothing. I could have forgotten I'd seen you until you reminded me.'

He had said she was unforgettable, and *he* most certainly was, but she managed a cool, dismissive expression, sitting there, hands looped around her ankles as he lounged beside her shirtless and smiling.

'You don't think that's possible, do you?' she said tartly. 'You think you're the man no woman could forget. And do stop laughing, because I am getting very bored with this situation.'

'It's livening up,' he said and she saw what he was looking at. Or rather who. Giles was coming towards them over the newly cut grass. 'Now's your chance to tell him,' said Matt.

# CHAPTER FIVE

MAYBE Lucy should have stayed where she was, sitting on the grass. Scrambling up looked like guilt and brushing her skirt down looked worse, but she did it automatically as soon as she saw Giles. Matt didn't move and Giles came striding towards them with an expression that could only be described as bullish.

She was neither writing an article nor nursing a headache; she was sprawling on the grass with a half-naked man, and Giles had every right to glare. She said brightly, 'Hello, darling. What are you doing here?'

To which he inevitably replied, 'What are you?'

'This is Matthew Lomas,' she said, playing for time. 'And this is Giles Lessing, my fiancé.'

The men acknowledged each other, Giles with a curt nod. Matt said, 'Congratulations,' without making it clear who he was congratulating.

'Matthew has been cutting the lawn for me,' Lucy babbled on. 'Old Joe's on holiday and he's been cutting Aunt Maud's grass. Have you finished that?'

'All done,' he said.

'Well, he's nearly finished the lawn,' said Lucy.

'Well,' said Giles, 'get on with it, my man.' Matt got up; taller, broader than Giles; the idea of him being anyone's man but his own was absurd.

She said, 'We've run out of petrol, and Matthew isn't a gardener. He's staying at Aunt Maud's while she decides whether to sell him the cottage on Strona.'

She could not get out the words 'where we met in May', although she half expected Matt to say that.

85

Instead he said, 'I'm painting the schoolroom for her now and hoping she'll knock it off the price.' He picked up his shirt. 'She's thinking of turning it into a museum.'

Lucy yelped 'A *what*?'

'A small museum of local history and local trades.'

Giles looked at Lucy, who shrugged. 'First I've heard of it.'

'Sounds a crackbrained scheme,' said Giles.

'Whose idea was that?' asked Lucy.

'You'd better come down and ask her. Nice to have met you,' he said affably to Giles. 'I've heard a lot about you.'

Giles didn't know what to make of that. He grunted in reply and Matt strode off across the lawn. 'What's he mean, he's heard a lot about me?' Giles muttered 'From you?'

'From Aunt Maud,' said Lucy. That was probably true, even if it was part of a lie.

'And he's staying with her? Does she know him?'

'He wants to buy her cottage.'

'So you've told me.' Giles was getting impatient. 'But what does she know about him, apart from that?'

'Not much.' The knowing was all on Matt's side, and since he had arrived in Edgeford Aunt Maud had been filling in the gaps for him. Now it seemed she had plans for the schoolroom that Lucy suspected would include Matt.

'I don't like him,' Giles declared. 'He's not the kind I'd let into my home. A very rough type.' Distaste flickered across his face. He was miles off the mark in his assessment of Matt, but the dislike was instinctive and just as Lucy had feared. 'I must say,' Giles warmed to his grievances, 'I didn't like coming round the house just now and seeing you there with him. I couldn't believe it.'

She could have said, 'We were only talking,' but her mind was full of other scenes and how Giles would have reacted to them. Bundled up in bed together, for instance, and how near she had come to taking as her lover the man Giles would not let into his home.

'Have you met him before?' he asked.

'At Aunt Maud's.' That was her chance of confession gone for ever. Now she would have to bluff it out.

'You didn't know he was coming here?'

'No.'

'She's always been foolish, your aunt,' said Giles. 'But I'd say she's overreached herself this time.'

Lucy bit back a denial that Aunt Maud was foolish. She could be very sensible, but on the other hand she could be wildly impractical and this idea of opening a museum posed problems. She said mildly, 'The room's big enough for a display centre and the house is so cluttered she could half fill it with what she's got. And she is a member of the local history society. They might like a little museum.'

'I'm not talking about the museum,' Giles snapped. 'I'm talking about that man she's taken in. I might have a word with her about him. After all, she is an old woman on her own.'

Lucy said, 'She wouldn't listen to you,' and Giles looked surprised and offended. He was not used to his opinions being ignored and Maud Beale had always greeted him affably. He had taken it for granted that she admired him and respected his judgment.

'She's stubborn as a mule,' said Lucy, because she was and because the last thing Lucy wanted was Giles getting involved in anything connected with Matt.

The sun was setting and greyness was creeping over

the garden. She wondered crazily what would happen if she ran after Matt. He wouldn't have got far. Out through the gates and a little way down Shady Lane. If she called him and ran and caught him up would the greyness brighten and birds start to sing again? She said, 'Let's go in, it's getting cold. What brought you?'

'You left in such a rush. When I told them you had a headache from too much sun mother said she thought I should come down and make sure you were all right.'

'That was sweet of her.'

Inside the house Giles said 'You are a goose, aren't you?' He drew her towards him and ruffled her hair. 'I can see I'll have to be keeping a close eye on you.'

'You will?' Her voice squeaked slightly.

'You're too naïve, my darling. Why do you think he stripped off his shirt?'

'Because it's sweating work shoving that old mower.'

Giles shook his head, smiling down at her. 'Showing off. He's a womaniser.'

'Maybe,' she said, although the sight of Matt stripped to the waist was hardly likely to shock her or surprise her.

'So you keep away from him,' said Giles. 'Promise me.'

'If I can.'

'Good girl. How's the headache?'

She had asked her mother that last night and Sylvia's headache had been an excuse, too, so that was something Lucy and her mother had in common. Giles's mother could start totting up if she knew. 'Still with me,' said Lucy, 'but under control.' She wished she could say the same about her life.

Giles stayed until her parents came home about half an hour later. They had been looking at the apartment Giles had told them about this morning and they were more than interested. They sat in the drawing-room, drinking coffee and talking about the advantages of modern plumbing and heating, while Giles told them about his plans for the top-floor conversion of Ivory Grange.

He was surprised that Lucy had not mentioned how it would be when they set up home together, and he went into details, just as he had last night with Matt practically within earshot. She would have done better to have stopped at Matt's table and introduced him as the man who had made an offer for the cottage. Giles had wanted to get out of the restaurant and might have taken some stopping, but Matt had been fully and rather well-dressed, so far as her brief glance could tell. Seeing him shirtless seemed to have convinced Giles that he was a thug on the make.

'Don't you like that idea?' asked Giles and she realised she was biting her lip and she might have been frowning. She had lost him half-way through his description of a room that would be a guest's bedroom. By now he could be anywhere; she hadn't been listening. She made herself smile and say, 'Of course,' and her mother said quickly,

'Of course you do. It all sounds delightful. Has she told you Aunt Maud's had an offer for the cottage in Scotland? We think she should sell it; it's never been any use to her. Another of Maud's mad ideas, although that one was a long time ago. She may be getting some sense in her old age, and taking the money.'

'Talking of mad ideas,' said Giles, 'did you know she's planning to open a museum?'

After a moment of astonishment they both laughed and said, '*What?*'

'In the old schoolroom,' said Giles.

Sylvia shrieked.

'What's she going to put in a museum, apart from herself?'

'A small local museum,' said Lucy. 'Local things, local crafts.'

'Who told you this?' asked Laurence.

'The man who might buy the cottage,' Giles said. 'He's staying at her house and working on the schoolroom. He was here just now.'

'Here? Why?' That was Sylvia, asking Lucy and then turning to Giles. It was Giles who answered, 'Mowing your lawn.'

'Aunt Maud sent him,' said Lucy, meeting their blank faces. 'He'd done her lawns and it would have been too much for Joe to tackle when he got back. So—Matthew came up.'

'Matthew?' Sylvia echoed softly, and Lucy wondered whether her own voice saying his name, had betrayed anything.

'Apparently Lucy had already met him at Miss Beale's,' said Giles and Lucy felt the apprehension in the air because there was no doubt about Giles's disapproval. 'I met him for the first time tonight. I was not impressed. I didn't like his manner at all. I hope he doesn't take advantage of the old girl.'

Or even of the young girl, thought Lucy, and felt her throat constrict, hysterical laughter rising in her. She said shakily, 'We ran out of petrol. A pity because the mower was going well.'

'Will he be back?' Sylvia's concern came over sharply.

'I don't know,' said Lucy.

'I strongly advise against it,' said Giles. 'He struck me as a rough type, a tough customer. I'll send one of our gardeners down.' They both thanked him and Lucy wondered what would happen if she said, 'You're a fine upstanding man yourself. What about you pushing the mower?' She imagined Giles, shirtless and pink-skinned, puffing as he pushed, and this time a giggle surfaced, and Giles asked, 'What's the joke?'

She coughed. 'Just a tickle in my throat. That would be very kind, if you could get the grass cut. It would be a big help.'

'You should have mentioned it,' said Giles. He glanced at his watch. 'I must be going.' He kissed Sylvia, and Laurence got up and put an affectionate arm around his shoulders, saying,

'Goodnight, my boy. We really appreciate what you're doing for us.'

He didn't mean the grass cutting. He meant taking the Gables off their hands and finding them a luxury apartment that was a bargain, because their daughter was marrying the son of Sir George Lessing.

So do I appreciate it, thought Lucy as she went with Giles to his car and he kissed her goodbye. She was in his debt and she must not begin to wonder if the price she would pay was too high.

'What the hell was that all about?' her father demanded when she came back into the drawing-room. He was flushed now and so was Sylvia, two bright spots of colour on her cheekbones. The moment the door closed on Lucy and Giles they must have started to panic. 'What's been going on? What did he say to Giles?'

'Who *is* he?' shrilled Sylvia. 'You never mentioned him.'

Lucy said quietly like someone repeating a lesson, 'He's the man who wants to buy the cottage. He's staying at Aunt Maud's while she makes up her mind. He's painting the old schoolroom and he's been doing the garden and she must have suggested he came up here and cut our lawns.'

Her father gave a bark of laughter. 'Maud sent him to mow the lawns? When has Maud ever bothered about our grass growing?'

Her mother asked, as if she dreaded the answer 'Is he—this Matthew—a good-looking man?' If Lucy had said no it might have put Sylvia's mind at rest but it would have been a very clumsy lie.

'Yes,' was the only answer she could give.

'Did he come up here to see you?' Her father again. 'And what did he say to Giles? Giles didn't like his manner. What manner? Just what did go on out there?' He was hectoring her as if he was in court and out to break down someone in the witness box. It would be too cruel to tell them about Strona, but he deserved a shock.

She looked him straight in the eyes, with a challenge he had never seen in her before. 'I'll tell you what happened,' she said. 'I came back from Giles's home and I was trying to get the mower going myself when Matt walked in.' She saw her mother's lips frame 'Matt', and she went on, 'So he took over. He mowed the lawn, and we were sitting talking under the cedar tree when Giles arrived. Giles's manner wasn't all that good. He told Matt to get on with the mowing and what seemed to have worried him most was that Matt had taken off his shirt and that he's quite a hunk. There wasn't much talking. A couple of minutes at most. No rowing, nothing like that. It was all low key, but Giles took an instant dislike to Matt.'

'You didn't?' said Sylvia.

'No.'

Her mother looked across at her father, signalling leave this to me, and Laurence Gillingham marched out of the room like a man who has to move fast before he loses his temper. Sylvia tried to pour herself more coffee but the pot was empty. She picked up her cup with dregs in it and turned it in her hands, reminding Lucy of Aunt Maud reading the tea leaves. 'You wouldn't do anything silly, would you?' she said.

'Like what?'

'Don't be so aggravating. You know what I'm talking about. Like letting this man get ideas about you. If he was attracted to you I don't say Aunt Maud wouldn't encourage him; she can be a real old fool and Giles was pretty mad just now.'

'I noticed,' said Lucy.

Sylvia set down the cup again with a bang that rattled it in the saucer. 'Well, keep away from him,' she ordered, 'and keep away from Aunt Maud, too. She's cracked enough to be certified and I'm beginning to wonder if you've got the sense you were born with.'

Rows in this house were commonplace but Lucy was in the middle of this one. She turned to go. She couldn't stand here being reviled and accused.

'Lucy,' her mother called. 'Oh, *please*,' and she had to look back.

Sylvia's eyes were brimming with tears. She blinked her lashes, as long and dark as Lucy's own, and a tear rolled down her cheek. 'You can't know what it means to us,' she said, 'getting out of this house and getting some real money for it, and we're so pleased that you're marrying Giles. Don't spoil it. Please show some sense and don't let it look as though you're playing around or Giles's mother could finish things.' Sylvia was scared, and pleading.

'I do know the score,' said Lucy, 'and I would be a fool to get on the wrong side of Giles's mother. She gave me a lecture today about how much she hates scandal and how she hoped being popular and lively doesn't run in the family.'

'Oh,' said Sylvia, getting the meaning of that.

Lucy immediately relented and smiled, saying, 'Don't worry. It isn't going to happen.'

In her bedroom, that phrase ran through her head like a recurring refrain . . . it isn't going to happen, nothing is going to happen . . . and she felt alone and lonely like an old woman who had missed all her chances of happiness.

In the morning she couldn't shake off her depression. She made up and dressed and she looked bright enough, but she felt drained, as if her sparkle and exuberance had gone.

Once again her mother and father were downstairs before her, and they both put on expressions of determined cheerfulness when she walked into the kitchen. Her father cleared his throat. 'Made a bit of an ass of myself last night. There was no call to start bawling you out. Sorry, poppet.'

Apologies from her father were something new and Lucy said, 'That's all right.'

'Somebody should see Maud,' said Sylvia. 'Giles knows what he's talking about. He's a businessman, and if he thinks that man might be conning her somebody ought to do something about it.'

Lucy couldn't resist 'Shall I?' and both of them practically leapt on her. Lucy was to keep away. It was her father her mother meant, not Lucy. Laurence had a busy day ahead of him, a busy week, but he would try to make time to go down to the Old Schoolhouse. Now though, he had to be off to the office. He drained his coffee and put down the empty cup by the plate with the toast crumbs and the smear of marmalade. Lucy could hardly remember them breakfasting together, and now it was two successive mornings.

'I hate this kitchen,' her mother said. It was old-fashioned, but it did get the morning sun; the breakfast room had damp patches. 'I'm going over to the apartment again today to get some ideas for curtains and carpets. I'm really going to enjoy that. Why don't you come with me?'

'I can't. I'm working.'

Her mother pulled a face, 'That little job of yours doesn't matter now.'

Perhaps not, but she needed the routine of it. While she was working she knew exactly what she was doing.

Lucy spent the morning calling on her customers, discussing their adverts, showing them artwork suggestions, and mid-afternoon she was sitting at her table making notes when Jackie whistled softly and hissed, 'I saw him first.'

Lucy looked up and felt as if she had stepped into a lift shaft. Matt had just walked in. The office was crowded and noisy and Kathleen, who had the most imposing desk as head of department, was looking enquiringly at him. The full length of the room was between Kathleen's desk and the table where Lucy and Jackie worked. Lucy couldn't hear what was being said but she was not the only one watching; every female head had turned. 'Who is *that*?' gurgled Jackie.

She didn't expect an answer; she expected him to be a stranger to Lucy, too. Lucy would have liked to scream, 'Get out of here,' because whatever excuse he had he *was* following her. He spoke for a few minutes. Kathleen listened, then called, 'Lucy', and Lucy got up.

Matt watched her walking towards him, moving between the desks, and for the life of her she couldn't break the eye contact even when she reached Kathleen's desk and was right beside him. 'You didn't tell us Miss Beale was opening a local museum,' said Kathleen.

Lucy shrugged. It was an effort to turn her head towards Kathleen. 'I don't know much about it. She's having the schoolroom painted and she's probably going to put some of her oddments in it and call it a museum. But you know Aunt Maud, it could end up as a strip club.'

Kathleen laughed. 'Get along with you. It sounds interesting. She wants an ad in for the next four weeks asking for bygones.'

'She shouldn't be buying more junk,' said Lucy.

'If it's junk,' said Matt, 'it should come cheap, although she's hoping for donations: old photographs, turn out your attics and cellars and see what you come up with. A collecting box for charity at the door. The local history society are meeting tonight and I've come to see about getting in a notice asking anyone interested to contact her.'

'Why not?' said Lucy tartly. 'The more the merrier.'

Kathleen's eyebrows rose because Lucy was not usually snappish. A display of instant hostility would start tongues wagging, so Lucy forced a smile. 'Do you know each other?' asked Kathleen.

There was silence and then Matt said, 'Hardly at all. I'm doing some work on the old schoolroom.'

'Lucy must do a little write-up for next week's edition,' said Kathleen. 'Then if the museum gets off the ground we'll do a real feature.' Lucy's lips parted to say something that would get her out of that, but there was nothing she could say. She was the obvious choice, so she said, 'Sure.'

'I'll give you some details,' said Matt.

'Thanks. You're the expert on antiques aren't you? Especially Staffordshire pottery.'

'Marvellous stuff,' he said. 'I can't get enough of it.'

By now everybody was watching them. Voices were hushed and when a phone rang it sounded unnaturally loud and the woman who answered it could be heard all over the room.

Lucy sat down at her table and Matt stood just behind her, leaning against the wall. She wished there had been a spare chair because this meant that he was looking down at her, which was almost as disturbing as if he was touching the nape of her neck. She turned a page of her notebook, reached for a ballpoint pen and asked, 'What exactly is she aiming for?'

'A small museum of local interests.' She wrote that down. 'Somebody called Bernard Beddows is preparing a map of the town at the turn of the century, naming shops and landmarks.' She made a note of that, too. She was having her work cut out keeping the writing steady, and when she did glance up it was to see Jackie, chin cupped in her hands, listening raptly as though she was thrilled to bits by these plans for the old schoolroom.

In fact Lucy could think of nothing less likely to interest Jackie than a museum. Matt was the attraction, his lazy voice, his striking looks. Meeting Lucy's ironic gaze, Jackie grinned and looked back at Matt and said, 'It sounds fascinating. A little museum; what a smashing idea. I wonder how I could help. By the way, I'm Jackie Allen. Who are you?'

'Matthew Lomas.'

'You're new in town?'

'Yes. I'm painting the schoolroom for Miss Beale.'

'And staying in the Old Schoolhouse,' Lucy said grimly.

'Are you two old friends?' Jackie couldn't credit Lucy having a friend like this and never mentioning him, but there did seem to be something between them, some sort of tension. She was dying to hear all about him, especially what plans he had for passing the time besides painting the old schoolroom.

'We met at Miss Beale's on Friday,' he said and Jackie said 'Really?' as if that was good news. Anyone could tell what she was thinking and hoping. Next she'd be asking if his family lived near here—like his wife? But Lucy hoped her friends would not get too friendly with Matt. If they did he might talk, or at least decide not to move on too soon.

She shut her notebook and stood up. 'I should be asking Aunt Maud about this. Are you coming?'

She didn't need to look back. She knew he was right behind her and that as soon as they left the room everybody would start talking. On her way down the stairs she said, 'There was no need to turn up at the office. She could have phoned that ad in.'

'I suppose she could. But then I wouldn't have seen where you worked.'

Out in the street she made for Aunt Maud's. 'Which is none of your business.'

'Good crowd are they, your workmates?'

'I get on with them all very well. Especially with Jackie.'

'The one fascinated by museums who wondered how she could help?'

'The one who was wondering how she could find out if you're married.'

'You can tell her,' he said, 'only on Strona.'

She was darting across the main road when he said that and it brought her to a sudden standstill so that a van braked. Matt gripped her elbow and yanked her out of the way. 'Let's live,' he said.

'What do you mean, only on Strona? Are you going to tell anyone that?'

'No.' But he still held her elbow.

She muttered through clenched teeth. 'Let go of me,' and looked around instinctively to see if anyone she knew was watching them.

He put his hands in his pockets and drawled, 'Sorry, ma'am. Next time I'll let the bloody van hit you.'

'I might have preferred that,' she said idiotically.

Aunt Maud's front door was ajar and the smell of new paint reached Lucy as she walked in. She followed the sound of voices into the parlour where Maud Beale was in conference with two of her cronies: a woman who was almost bouncing up and down in her chair with enthusiasm, and Bernard Beddows, retired bank manager and chairman of the local history society.

Lucy was drawn into their happy circle. They couldn't wait to get started on Maud's new project and tonight the society was having a meeting and Lucy would be coming, of course. Matt had not followed her into the room but she was sure he would be at the meeting.

If somebody else had been painting the schoolroom Lucy would have thought it was all quite a lark. It was going to provide Aunt Maud and her friends with action and interest. Lucy could hardly complain that it would be too much for Aunt Maud because she never had any trouble recruiting helpers, and if it didn't work out she could always close down and hand back the exhibits.

But Matt was involved, so Lucy was racking her brains to think of arguments against. She said, 'Don't overdo it and don't go buying things you can't afford.'

She was talking to Aunt Maud, but Bernard Beddows cleared his throat, reminding Lucy that he was Maud's financial adviser and could be relied on to watch her interests. 'What's it going to cost to turn the schoolroom into a display centre?' Lucy persisted. 'You can't just paint the walls and call it a museum.'

'Come and see.' Maud Beale swept out of the parlour, gleeful as a child with a new toy, opening the door from the wide entrance hall into the old schoolroom. In there the junk had been moved to one side, and there were ladders, brushes, tins. The ceiling between the high arched beams and the walls had been painted pale peach. It was an improvement on the psychedelics.

'Very pretty,' said Lucy. 'Did he do it?'

'Matthew? Yes. And when I saw how nicely it was coming on I thought it's always been wasted space and I should be using it for something.' She had bought this property fifty years ago, and planned to open an antique shop with the man she was going to marry. But he had died when a ship sank and the old schoolroom had never had a real purpose. 'Matthew suggested a museum,' she said.

'What has it got to do with him?'

Maud Beale chuckled. 'Well, I've always been a magpie; I've collected enough to fill a museum. And you were asking how much this is going to cost? Now that's Matthew again. That's what he does. He's a builder and a carpenter; he can do everything we need doing in here.'

'For how much?'

'Bernard says we're getting him cheap. Matthew says he'll enjoy doing it and I think we're lucky.'

'I think lucky is not the word,' Lucy muttered. 'He's too handy by half. Gardener, builder. He came up and did our lawn—you know that?' Aunt Maud did.

'And I'm glad Giles didn't hear what Matt told me you'd said, that I could be marrying him for security. I don't know what you were thinking of, showing Matt those old photographs and telling him I was a deprived child who nobody loved.'

'Did I say that?' Maud seemed to be finding a flaw in the perfect paintwork of one of the walls. She was frowning at that rather than facing Lucy. 'Well,' she said truculently, 'his mother does choose his girlfriends.'

'You never said that as well?' Lucy would never have believed that Aunt Maud could be so indiscreet.

'Now that is true,' which Maud Beale seemed to consider all the defence she needed. 'Poor Charlotte Machim got her marching orders because she'd seen a bit of life before Giles started taking an interest in her.'

'But that was years ago.' Charlotte, a beauty queen with a roving eye, had been married and divorced and married again since then.

'And the girl who worked in their offices . . .' Aunt Maud seemed to know more about Giles's past than Lucy did '. . . her family wasn't good enough for her ladyship.'

'Stop it! I won't listen to another word.' Lucy had heard enough local gossip. 'Giles's mother has always been very nice to me and I like her very much, but if you want to wreck my life you're going the right way about it. I love Giles. You know that so why are you doing this?'

'But it took you so long to make up your mind.'

'So what's wrong with that?' Only long enough to make sure. She had her parents' example to prove that marriage should not be rushed.

'I knew as soon as I saw Martin,' said Maud Beale, 'that he was the one I could have lived with all my life.' She had lived her life alone but Lucy could imagine the girl she used to be, too heavy-featured for beauty and yet beautiful.

There was a photograph of her Martin upstairs by Maud's bed and Lucy said gently, 'I know.' She was going to insist, 'I do love Giles,' but Maud sighed and said,

'It was as though we knew each other so well. And that's how Matthew said he felt when he first saw you.'

That was Matthew's little joke. That was no first meeting in the green parlour on Friday night, and Lucy tasted bitterness like acid in her mouth. She could have said, 'We learned all but the naked truth of each other on Strona,' but she was glad now that she had told Aunt Maud nothing of that. It would only have made her more concerned that Giles might not be the love of Lucy's life. She could decide that Matt's finding Lucy and turning up like this was written in the stars. And although she liked Giles well enough she might think a dark handsome stranger was more romantic.

Lucy had to make the whole thing seem ridiculous. 'Well, I don't feel anything about him,' she said, 'except that he's a drifter with the gift of the gab, and he's got a nerve if he thinks I'd look twice at him.' Her scornful little laugh was genuine; she had summed him up neatly. She went on, 'He isn't half the man Giles is,' but thought she should stop there because that she was not so sure about. She said quickly, 'Giles disliked him so much that he made me promise to keep away from him. So long as he's here I shall stay away.'

'There's no need for that,' Aunt Maud protested but Lucy felt there was every need.

'Tell him to stop playing silly games,' she said. 'And you stop, too. No more talk like this, and I don't want you discussing Giles or me with him.' She patted Maud's shoulder, half hug, half a slight shake, and walked out of the old schoolroom hearing Maud sighing deeply.

I love Giles for all sorts of reasons, she reminded herself as she went towards the door, while Matt means nothing but trouble. There is no contest, but I am keeping away from him.

As she opened the door into the street she looked back. She had not meant to but it was as though someone called her name. Nobody had. There was only Matt in the hall at the bottom of the stairs and she knew he had not spoken. Neither of them moved. Their eyes met for a brief moment and oh, it was there, the pull between them that was drawing her towards him. She couldn't speak. It took all her strength to back off through the door and pull it shut behind her. She almost ran, dodging the walkers on the pavement, flashing quick smiles at folk she knew, and she was half-way home before she remembered her car in the office car park.

She didn't go into the office. She drove home, and by that time she was calm and in control again.

Next morning Jackie announced that she had attended the meeting of the local history society last night as press, and had volunteered to help almost any evening. Her eyes danced as she declared, 'It's a real turn-on, is that museum. Sexiest set-up I've seen for a long time.'

Jackie was a charmer, and if she made a dead set for Matt it might defuse the situation for Lucy. Of course there was no hint of jealousy in Lucy's flare of irritation, it was just that she did not wish to be reminded of Matt in any way. She said, 'I've got enough problems without getting involved in Aunt Maud's latest. Don't tell me anything about it, and you'd better write the write-up. Do you want to come to my engagement party on Sunday, round the swimming pool at the Lessings? Everybody bring a friend and a swimsuit.' There were five on the staff so that was ten guests for Lady Lessing's list.

It was true, Lucy did have enough to think about, what with the wedding and everything. She was not going near Matt; she was not letting herself think about him. She managed to keep those resolutions for the rest of the week.

On Friday Giles met her out of work and drove her

home. The weather was holding, the forecast for Sunday was fine and hot and Alys Lessing had supervised all the arrangements for the party. Giles was in good humour, telling Lucy about a deal his father had brought off and that they might soon be putting business in the way of her father's firm.

It all sounded encouraging, everything was going so smoothly. As they walked into the house there was this week's bouquet filling a bowl on one of the hall tables. Ever since he had started dating Lucy, Giles had sent her flowers. They came from the local florists and were always beautifully fresh so that sometimes the house seemed to be full of them. She had suggested he changed the order to a monthly one, but Giles had said they were charged to company expenses anyway so they might as well leave it as a standing weekly order.

Betty Miller, their help, was waiting, coat on, in the kitchen. She had been coming here for nearly a year, which was a record because staff rarely stayed long. Usually they left, saying that Mrs Gillingham was all right but you never knew where you were with her from one day to the next. But they all liked Lucy.

Betty greeted her with, 'Your mother isn't back yet.' So Betty had been kept hanging around because Sylvia had not settled up with her before she went out. This often happened and it was thoughtless. Lucy dived into her purse and apologised and Betty said that was all right, only she wanted to catch the shops.

'The roses came,' she said. 'I put them in the blue bowl and I took last week's lot into the drawing-room.' Giles was still in the hall, and Betty looked through at him and the flowers. 'Beautiful, aren't they? I think he's lovely. You are lucky.' Then she hurried off with her shopping basket.

'Will you have a cup of tea?' Lucy asked Giles. I'm

just making myself one.'

'Tea would be fine,' he said, and she brewed a pot and carried it into the drawing-room. He took the cup she was offering him, milked and sugared to his taste, and suddenly she was remembering the island. The cottage was as rough as this room was elegant, but the memory filled her with the piercing pain of homesickness. These porcelain cups were eggshell thin; there they had drunk from mugs. Giles put down his cup and took a ring case from his pocket; this man, with his smooth pink hands, was a different breed from the man she had married in the ring of rock.

'Let's see if it fits this time,' said Giles. It was a very fine ring. He admired it himself, holding it so that it caught the light before he reached for Lucy's hand. But she couldn't lift her hand and give it to him. It lay heavy and cold and he had to lean across. He smiled, squeezing her fingers, and now of course it was a perfect fit. 'It looks good on you,' he said.

This was the kind of ring that was phoney ninety-nine times out of a hundred, but not when it had belonged to Giles's grandmother. Lucy had a small fortune on her finger. She said, 'It's gorgeous but I'll be terrified of losing it. Or suppose a stone falls out?'

'It's insured, of course, and why should you lose it? I want you to wear it; you'll soon get used to it.' He sat back, looking at her approvingly. 'My mother has some very fine pieces and some of them will suit you very well.' Lucy had a crazy vision of herself standing like a Christmas tree being circled by Giles and Lady Lessing, who were pinning and draping baubles on her.

She said, 'Heaven knows what they'll say to this at work.'

Giles picked up his cup of tea again. 'I do think you should be handing in your notice there. What with the wedding preparations and getting our home ready, you'll have plenty to do. I don't want you worn out before the wedding.'

The wedding was months away. She would miss her workmates and clients; she didn't want to leave until she had to. 'My mother agrees,' said Giles, as if that should clinch it.

Lucy murmured, with a flash of mischief, 'I could always give Aunt Maud a hand with the museum.'

'Don't be silly, darling,' said Giles pompously, and for the second time she bit back, 'Don't be stuffy.' She should be ashamed of herself. She couldn't resign just like that, but Giles only wanted her to give up her job because he was considerate, and she must not be ungrateful. She took the teacup out of his hands and put it on the floor and put her arms around his neck. 'You are a very nice man,' she said. 'I'm very lucky.'

He kissed her warmly but without passion. After all, it was still broad daylight and the doors were open, and when the phone rang it was disturbing nothing. If it had been Lucy would have let it ring, but at the second burr Giles said, 'The phone,' as if she might have gone deaf.

'So it is,' she said.

The caller was someone she had invited to the engagement party, asking about wedding gifts, and if the list was ready because they didn't want to duplicate. Lucy stalled, thanking the woman who was her parents' friend rather than hers. 'We haven't got round to anything like that yet, but we're looking forward to seeing you on Sunday.'

'Such a lovely house,' burbled the woman, 'and such nice people, the Lessings. It will be the wedding of the year round here. You *have* done well.'

Somebody is going to say that very soon, thought Lucy, and I am going to scream. This time she said,

'Thank you. Well, goodbye till Sunday.' She put down the phone just as her father opened the front door.

Giles's car outside had been enough to cheer up Laurence Gillingham and he went straight into the drawing-room to greet him. 'What's she giving you? Tea? Have a real drink, my boy.'

Giles gave a smiling refusal. 'I may be driving.' But Laurence Gillingham went to the rosewood cabinet that housed bottles and poured himself a generous Scotch. He took several gulps before he sat down and declared, 'I needed that.'

'Bad day?' asked Lucy.

'A long one,' her father said.

She wondered if he was drinking more these days. He had always been a moderately heavy social drinker, although he could hold it; she had never seen him make a fool of himself. But he had knocked back that whisky as if he really needed it.

'Look.' She held out her hand so that her father could not miss her ring, and he almost spilled the little whisky remaining in his glass leaning forward to admire it.

'That is a very handsome ring.'

'My grandmother's,' said Giles as if it still belonged to her, and Lucy thought, she'd have to wear it on her thumb now it's been stretched to fit my working woman's hands.

Her father and Giles were carrying on like a mutual admiration society, her father saying that Giles was exactly the man he would have chosen for his daughter and Giles declaring that Laurence Gillingham would be a father-in-law in a million. They both exuded satisfaction.

Of course Lucy was included in all this. Her father kissed her and said that she was going to make Giles as proud of her as he had always been—that was a laugh, although she was sure he believed it now. And Giles kept an arm around her, holding her close to his side.

She looked down at the flashing ring on her rather grubby hand and said, 'I must wash and freshen up. I did come straight from work and there were some last-minute flaps. It's usually a bit sticky and tacky on Fridays.'

'Don't be long,' said her father and Giles said that she always looked fresh as a daisy. She ran upstairs and shut her bedroom door. She took off her ring and left it on the dressing-table before she went into the bathroom.

Her father and Giles would find things to talk about and when her mother came home she would join in, adding her gaiety to the happy scene. Or she could dash up here demanding to be shown the ring, and that would please her because five big diamonds were more than your average engagement ring.

Lucy got into the bath instead of showering, adding a herbal essence and swishing it around, pinning her hair high because she could hardly excuse taking time to wash and dry it before she went down again. She was going deliberately slowly. She wished she could be alone for a while, although she had no more decisions to make, no options left. Now she had to pretty herself and go downstairs wearing Giles's grandmother's ring.

She put the ring on last of all. After dressing and making up and brushing her hair she slid it on her finger, and looked at her reflection: tip-tilted green eyes and wide soft-lipped mouth. It was a sensuous mouth, she supposed. Her lipstick toned with her golden tan and coppery hair, and she ran the point of her tongue between her lips, tasting the faint perfume. Then she said aloud, 'I wouldn't have said I looked like a daisy.'

Her mother was home. It was her voice Lucy heard as she came down the stairs. Lucy had a smile on her lips.

She had smiled wryly at her own silly joke before the mirror and kept the smile there so that she walked into the drawing-room looking how they expected to see her. 'Show me,' her mother gushed. She took Lucy's hand and went into transports of delight. 'Oh, that is gorgeous!'

'My grandmother's,' said Giles smugly.

'An heirloom, of course,' said Sylvia.

'Can I have my keeper back?' asked Lucy and Giles clapped hands to his pockets.

'Sorry, I'd forgotten that.' He had to hunt for it and Lucy heard herself say,

'My grandmother's,' because, although its value didn't compare with the diamond ring, it had belonged to her father's mother, Aunt Maud's sister, and she liked it and wanted it. When Giles finally fished it out she put it back on her right hand.

'Giles has been telling us,' said her father, 'that he thinks you should give up your job.'

'There's no hurry,' said Lucy.

'I wouldn't say that.' Her father was opening a bottle of wine. He poured a little, sniffed and tasted, and, appearing satisfied, began to fill glasses. Lucy wondered who he would have complained to if it had been corked. 'From what I hear the next few months are going to be hectic. Your new home, for instance.'

'I won't be doing the building, will I?' said Lucy and she could understand Giles's irritation.

'Well, of course you won't, darling, but there are plenty of things you'll be consulted on.'

Like carpets and curtains and décor and design. But the plans were drawn up and would be approved. When Giles had described their apartment it had sounded like a *fait accompli*, and Lucy knew that she would not be expected to have an opinion that did not coincide with

Alys Lessing's choice. She didn't mind much. It would be a fantastic home and she would be lucky to be living in it. As everybody kept telling her, she had done very well for herself.

They talked about the party on Sunday, who was coming and how fortunate they were with the weather. And about the wedding. 'The reception at my home, we thought,' said Giles. 'If that's all right with you.'

By May her parents wouldn't be living here, and Ivory Grange would make a superb setting. 'Lovely,' said Sylvia.

Lucy kept smiling and Giles kept an arm around her. They were all enjoying themselves. Her father told funny stories about weddings he had attended and her mother played up to Giles, pealing with laughter at his jokes. It was all very merry and Lucy kept smiling.

But time went slowly for her. It was plain that she and Giles were going nowhere else tonight, so she went into the kitchen and got a meal together out of the freezer. They ate sitting around the dining-room table.

When the clock in the hall chimed eleven Giles looked at his watch, eyebrows rising, and said, 'I never realised it was that late.' Lucy thought, I would have believed dawn should be breaking, but her mother and father both seemed genuinely astonished. Sylvia was still lively and chattering, making a token show of helping with the washing up after Giles had left and Laurence had gone upstairs.

What she would be wearing on Sunday was still occupying Sylvia's mind, whether she should buy something new tomorrow, and Lucy went patiently over at least a dozen things hanging in her mother's wardrobe that would be striking and suitable.

Grudgingly Sylvia agreed, but immediately brightened at the prospect of wedding outfits. 'I shall certainly go to town for that. You'll be in white, of course.'

'I've already been measured for the veil,' said Lucy. 'Another heirloom, and going off-white if that means anything.'

Sylvia giggled behind her hand, 'If it does, keep quiet about it.' She sobered at once, 'Oh, it's such a comfort to know you're safe with Giles. He's really a man you can trust, and he idolises you, he told us. Or did he say idealise? Well, they're both the same thing, aren't they?'

'No, they are not,' said Lucy. She thought it would be idealise and that was not as comforting as her mother imagined.

She took off her ring before she went to bed and put it on the dressing-table. Next morning it was waiting for her. It was the kind of ring you felt you should dress up to; with Lucy's casual Saturday clothes of jeans and T-shirt it did look like a well-made fake, although everybody who knew the Lessings would know that Giles's bride would only be flashing around gems that were the real thing.

The *Herald* arrived with the morning papers. Lucy had seen all Fred's shots and been happiest with the one selected, which was a very good photograph indeed of Giles and herself. It was on the front page, across three columns, headlined by Kathleen 'Our ad-girl to wed local tycoon', and with some flattering copy about them both. Jackie's story, 'Local museum in old schoolhouse', was running on page three.

Lucy drank her coffee and ate a bowl of muesli with the picture of Giles smiling up at her. Her father came into the kitchen, admired the photograph and left to see a client. Her mother came down and went starry-eyed over it. Sylvia had an appointment with her hairdresser and would be taking the paper along, although nearly everybody would have seen it as the copies were given away.

'I'm going to the library,' said Lucy.

She had to invite Aunt Maud to this engagement party. Parties round swimming pools were hardly Aunt Maud's thing but she must be asked, so on her way to the library she would call at the Old Schoolhouse. Besides, she was curious to see how it was all working out.

Matt might not be there. If he was, there would be others around so she could keep her distance and somebody else between them. She did not want him getting the idea that she was so scared of him she dare not show her face.

She walked down into the town, which was full of Saturday morning shoppers, saying hello to the folk she knew. 'I liked your picture,' she was told, but she didn't stop to chat because she really did want to get down to Aunt Maud's and find out what was going on. And, as she expected, the answer was plenty.

Cars were parked all along the road outside the house. That wasn't unusual, parking was always tight in the middle of town especially on Saturdays, but she recognised several as belonging to Aunt Maud's friends, and as she reached them a woman popped up from behind the boot of her car carrying a cardboard box.

'Isn't this a splendid idea?' she called gaily, eyes shining behind her spectacles. 'I've brought a goffering iron and a pit pony's cap. Did you know there used to be a blacksmith's forge where my house is?'

'No, I didn't,' said Lucy. She followed the woman into the house. It looked as it had often done when Aunt Maud's committees were organising jumble sales: full of busy folk.

In the schoolroom the smell of paint was still pungent. A couple of students from the polytechnic were marking one wall into squares, and as Lucy walked in from the hall Aunt Maud swooped on her. 'I thought you'd be down today,' she said. 'That's where the plan's going to be. How Edgeford was at the turn of the century. Look at this.'

She handed Lucy a duplicated copy of a detailed piece of research on which the chairman of the history society must have spent months. There were houses and shops and small factories that had vanished long before Lucy was born. A roller-skating rink, that had become a picture palace then a bingo hall and was now a DIY store. Coalmines and brickworks were marked on the hills, and Gaskin's Wood, where the murder was.

'This was the village school, of course.' Aunt Maud jabbed with a forefinger. 'The houses in Shady Lane were just being built. There's yours.'

'And we're copying out the church births, marriages and deaths for 1900,' said the lady with the pit pony's cap, 'so that anyone with their roots here can come back and look up their family. That could be quite a tourist attraction, couldn't it?'

It could, in a small way. The history society had brought in their bygones, asked around among their friends, and in the parlour the chairman was accepting contributions and handing out receipts.

Matt came into the schoolroom. Lucy had her back to the door, standing with Aunt Maud pouring over the plan, but she knew he was there before she turned. The room was fairly full and most of them were chattering, but she *knew*. 'Hello,' she said, and she knew he was the reason she was here.

# CHAPTER SIX

MATT came across, wiping greasy hands on a paper towel, and Lucy asked 'What have you been up to?' in just the right casual tone.

'Putting a tandem together. Actually it's in good nick.'

'The 1900s were a bicycling age,' Aunt Maud declared. 'There was a local club called the Edgeford 'Ooligans.'

'Good grief,' said Lucy faintly.

'I hear your house is on the map,' said Matt.

'Ivory Grange is too far out,' said Aunt Maud. 'Where's this ring of yours?'

Lucy had her left hand in the pocket of her jeans. Now she rather reluctantly drew it out and the women gathered round because they all knew her and most of them knew the Lessings. There was a chorus of admiration. They had seen the newspaper, too, and they thought the picture was good, and when was the wedding going to be?

'In May,' said Lucy.

'We're hoping to open the museum in May,' said Aunt Maud.

'May is going to be a very busy month,' said Matt.

Sue, one of the art students, a thin, eager girl with her hair in rainbow colours, asked hopefully, 'Are you staying till then?'

'No,' he said and Lucy told herself that was a relief.

It was several minutes later that she found herself facing him and he said, 'I can understand why you're drooling at him in that photograph. You're thinking of the size of the ring.'

'Don't be absurd,' she said coolly.

Bernard Beddows came loping in, his bald head pink with excitement. He was waving a couple of brass rollers indented in fish shapes.

'Just look at these. Used for making sweets,' he informed them, 'in the boiling room behind the Beehive Stores in Market Street. Mrs Hodkiss has just brought them in. Aren't they a pretty pair?'

'Come and see my etchings,' hissed Matt out of the corner of his mouth.

'Your what?' said Lucy.

'The tandem.'

While everybody was admiring the brass rollers she asked Aunt Maud about the party. Aunt Maud said she'd heard all about it but her rheumatism played up by swimming pools. 'Well, it will be rather a crush,' said Lucy, and she went with Matt into the garden. The shed door was open and the two-seater bicycle did look well preserved.

'Does it go?' she asked.

'I was just going to try it out. Shall we?'

He wheeled it on to the grass. The garden was all lawn and trees, apart from a few flower beds. There was space enough to cycle around but Lucy hesitated and Sue, who had followed them, darted forward squealing, 'Let me! I've been dying to ride on this.'

'You can have the next trip,' said Lucy, managing to get astride. The saddle was hard and she had difficulty keeping her feet on the pedals. Then they were away, wobbling and weaving. The pedals were going furiously and she clutched the handlebars and kept her head down. They circled the flower beds, narrowly missing the trees, with Lucy lurching from side to side and never quite getting her balance.

When her feet slipped from the pedals she kept them turned out and stuck out, and Matt pedalled on between the trees at the bottom of the garden, until she shrieked, 'I'm falling,' and toppled into the long grass. It could easily have been the other way, into the nettles.

'Are you all right?' Matt propped the bike against a tree and reached a hand to help her to her feet and she began to laugh.

'First time I've been on a bike, let alone a tandem.'

'I believe you.' His grip pressed the ring, making her wince. Sue came between the trees smirking and said happily, 'You came a cropper.'

Lucy had landed hard enough to knock the air out of her and she gulped for breath. 'It's bad enough getting on and off in these; those long skirts must have been murder.'

'My turn now,' said Sue.

'Later,' said Matt. He wheeled the bike away and Sue skipped along beside him. Lucy stayed where she was, brushing the grass from her knees and bottom. She seemed to do a lot of that when she was around Matt. He put the bike into the shed and Sue went on talking, her rainbow head a bobbing splash of colour. Outside the shed she put a hand on his arm but Matt turned her towards the house and walked back to Lucy.

'Watch it,' she said when he reached her. 'She can't be a day over fourteen.'

'She's nineteen.'

'Don't bank on it,' she said darkly, although she knew it for a fact.

He looked towards the gate in the wall. 'Shall we leave them to it?'

'I do have other things to do but I don't need company.'

He pulled the rusty bolt and lifted the latch; the hinges creaked because this gate was not used much. 'Let's walk over the moors. They're almost like Strona.' He caught her hand again and she could feel the life force flowing into her. Her fingers wanted to stay laced in his hand and her feet wanted to run with him.

'Come with me?' he said, but she jerked her hand away.

'I'm going nowhere with you. By all means take a walk over the hills yourself, and if you come to a mineshaft, drop in.'

Silly, childish talk! How stupid she sounded! She went back into the house and through the hall, calling goodbyes and almost bumping into Jackie who was coming out of the parlour.

'Small world,' said Jackie. 'Thought I'd call in.' She gave Lucy a knowing grin. 'Where is he?'

'He was in the garden,' said Lucy. 'And if you want a ride on his tandem you'll have to join the queue. The one in there with rainbow hair is first.'

'Eh?' said Jackie. Lucy laughed, and went out of the house still laughing although she was not particularly amused.

It was a small world all right. In the library she walked slap-bang into Charlotte Machin-that-was. It was some time since they had seen each other and Charlotte's congratulations seemed genuine. Her eyes gleamed when she saw the ring but there was a little glitter of malice in them when she advised Lucy, 'Don't choose the steamy stuff. Alys Lessing wouldn't like it.' She was talking about library books and Lucy couldn't think of a reply. Charlotte added, 'I wish you luck, it's Snow White they want up there. But then I suppose you are, aren't you?'

Lucy took out a book called *Passion's Price* with a cover

of writhing nudes, which was hardly her taste, because
Charlotte made her feel prudish, but she proved herself
not a prude but an idiot.

Her mother was home when she got back. 'Been to the
library, darling, what did you get?' and when Lucy
showed her Sylvia's eyes widened. She did not like the
look of that. If Lucy was developing a taste for sexy
books Sylvia could not believe that she was fantasising
about Giles.

Lucy was not fantasising about anybody. She was
keeping a rein on her thoughts and her emotions. She
skimmed through the rest of the day, superficially
serene, talking and smiling. Three of her mother's
friends called that evening and went into raptures over
the ring, and when Sylvia told them the house was as
good as sold, they thought it was *such* a good idea that
Lessing Electronics should take it over.

During the evening Giles phoned and he and Lucy
talked for a while. He was collecting her after breakfast
because she was the hostess at this party, although all she
had to do was tell his mother who she had invited. 'I
can't believe our luck with the weather,' he said. 'It's
going to be another beautiful day.'

'Of course it is,' said Lucy. Later, as she lay in bed
waiting for sleep, the heat was as oppressive as a blanket
over her head, and some instinct seemed to be warning
her that a storm that had nothing to do with the weather
was coming ...

Usually Lucy liked parties. She was good company,
good fun, and usually she had a good time. But she was
apprehensive about this one, although her friends were
coming, and those who would be her friends when she
was Lucinda Lessing. Nothing could go wrong with the
arrangements, nothing would dare; Alys always used
the same caterers and her household staff were paragons

of efficiency. But Lucy got ready in the morning feeling
that she should be keeping her fingers crossed.

She was wearing a multi-coloured sundress and
taking a yellow swimsuit. When she was ready she let
herself out of the house and sat on the stone seat by the
marble statue waiting for Giles. He had kept his word
about getting the lawns mowed for them, sending down
both a gardener and an up-to-date mower. The grounds
of the Gables looked better than she could ever
remember and she felt a little regret that bulldozers
would probably be ploughing and razing before long.
The future of the mock-Grecian lady was uncertain, too.
Lucy's parents would hardly be taking her along to their
modern apartment. Perhaps a spot could be found for
her in the acres of Ivory Grange. In gardens that size she
would hardly be noticed.

'Loocee,' her mother carolled as she came tripping
across the lawn. 'I thought you'd gone.' Sylvia was in a
shell-pink kimono, her hair drawn back in a bandeau of
the same colour and her face gleaming with a moisturis-
ing cream. 'I still can't make up my mind what to wear.'
She sounded as if this was a momentous matter.

Lucy said firmly, 'The white dress,' because she was
not getting into that again.

'You really think so?' Sylvia was doubtful but when
Lucy said, 'Giles will be here any minute,' she scurried
back into the house to put on the rest of her make-up
before facing anyone else.

Giles did arrive before long. The sun was well up.
They could not have ordered a better day. This summer
had been mostly golden days, and there was the old
saying 'happy the bride the sun shines on', which might
work as well for brides-to-be, but sitting beside Giles,
skimming along, Lucy found herself scanning the blue
skies for clouds.

She had been to parties at Ivory Grange before. Dinner parties, coffee mornings, parties around the pool. But she was the star attraction at this one, and Giles's mother gave her a quick glance that took it all in, from shining copper hair to toenails painted bronze in strap sandals, before she smiled and kissed her and told her how pretty she looked.

Alys was in the orangery, an ornate glasshouse as old as the house. Italian statues and pots had been imported, their places unchanged for over two hundred years, and now palm trees grew high, masses of fuchsias bloomed and honeysuckle and jasmine scented the air.

The buffet ran on centre tables down the centre of the orangery. Alys walked round, giving a final touch to flower arrangements, adjusting the lie of a spoon. One of the girls who was there to help with the waitressing had known Lucy for years, and as Lady Lessing swept by, regal as royalty, Diane winked at Lucy. Unfortunately Alys looked back at that moment, quelling Diane with a glare that almost convulsed Lucy.

Diane rolled her eyes skywards as Lucy walked on in Alys's wake, giving Diane a sympathetic grimace. She was here today to show everyone what a dutiful and suitable daughter-in-law she would be. She knew that. By accepting Giles's ring she had accepted that as part of the bargain.

The invitation was from mid-day until six o'clock, but Lucy's parents were expected earlier and their car was the first to arrive. Sylvia was wearing the white dress, a fine lawn, very simple and very expensive, although not so long ago she would not have taken Lucy's advice on clothes or anything else. As always she looked stunning.

Sir George and Laurence Gillingham hailed each other like brothers and George's eyes brightened at the sight of Sylvia. 'Ah, Sylvia, lovely as ever. It's easy to see where Lucy gets her looks.'

Lucy did not look much like either of them, and she knew that although Alys was smiling she would have preferred Sylvia's smile to be less seductive when she told George he was even more handsome than his handsome son.

Sylvia kissed Giles then and it was almost one happy family. 'George is set on making an announcement . . .' Alys sounded as if he was a small boy with a party piece '. . . so you and I will have to welcome the guests, Sylvia, and then Giles and Lucy will make their entrance at twelve o'clock.'

Like Cinderella in reverse, Lucy thought; and all the guests were here today because Lucy had won her prince. Her hand held in Giles's, she went with him to wait offstage until their cue came. They stood, shielded by the curtains of an upper window, watching the terrace fill with guests. She said, 'I suppose there's no chance of eloping?'

Giles laughed. 'The mothers would kill us.'

Mine wouldn't, she thought. Mine just wants me married to you, although, yes, she does want to buy a wedding outfit. 'We'll have to be patient,' he said, and kissed her without mussing her hair.

This was a room she had not been in before, a small parlour with watercolours on the walls. She looked at the pictures until Giles said, 'I should think they're all here. We'd better go down.' Now she had to face them and she tensed as Giles reached for her. 'All right?' he said, and she forced a smile.

'Stage fright.'

Of course, she was joking. Lucy got on well with people, but maybe today was different for her because she had moved up the social ladder. Giles would have indignantly denied being a snob, but he could understand Lucy being overawed at the prospect of stepping out now as his wife-to-be. 'Nothing to be frightened of.' He slipped her hand through his arm and patted it. 'I'll be right beside you; I'll always be with you.'

Alys was standing at one of the long drawing-room windows that opened on to the terrace, and as Giles and Lucy slipped into the room she hurried to meet them. 'Come on now, everybody's waiting for you.' She pushed the windows wide and George turned as his wife and son and Lucy came out of the house and stood beside him on the top step of the terrace.

It was *hot* out here. Everybody must be dying to get into the pool. The blue water shimmered and Lucy found herself staring at it rather than at the guests. The chatter was dying down because Sir George, perspiring in his lightweight suiting, was making hand signals for quiet.

When he got it, he boomed in his chairman-of-the-board voice, 'Thank you all for coming, it's good to see you. And now I've got a very pleasant announcement to make and you know what that is. We're welcoming a daughter into the family. Our little Lucy.' He gave her a fatherly hug. 'And she *is* our Lucy because she's agreed to marry this reprobate son of ours. Take him in hand, eh, m'dear? So, friends, I give you Giles and Lucy, and I hope you'll join me in toasting their long life and happiness.'

Corks started popping and all around Lucy glasses were being filled and raised. Among the voices she heard Jackie call, 'Good on you, Luce,' and she looked across the pool to where Jackie sat, raising the glass she had just taken from a tray being carried round. Matt stood beside her. Lucy should have known Jackie would bring him.

She had known. She had kept away from that window because she hadn't wanted to see him come. She drank from the glass she was holding herself, then realised that somebody had hold of her hand and was oohing and ahhing over her ring.

Then they had to move around, displaying the ring, getting congratulations from everybody. Some of the guests said they had been expecting it, which they probably had because Lucy and Giles had been going around together for a while and his parents obviously approved of the match. Nobody was surprised to hear that the newlyweds would be living in Ivory Grange. Lucy even overheard one woman say, 'She should do nicely, once Alys has got her trained.'

Lucy's own friends showed no cattiness; they were all delighted for her. Kathleen, who had come with her husband said, 'I hope this doesn't mean we'll be losing you too soon,' and Giles replied,

'Well, you know how it is.'

Jackie said, 'Aren't you lucky, coming into all this?' and Giles took no offence because he knew she was including him. Then he saw Matt and stopped smiling.

'I hope you don't mind, I'm representing Miss Beale,' said Matt.

'Of course not,' said Giles stiffly. 'You're welcome.'

'Thank you.' Matt held his glass. 'Long life,' he said, the toast Sir George had proposed. His eyes met Lucy's. 'And all the happiness you deserve.'

Lots of them said that, it was a cliché, and it was said this time in a warm, friendly fashion, but Lucy felt that the smiling face was a mask and the automatic thank-you died on her lips.

She moved on, Giles beside her muttering, 'What's he doing here? Why should Miss Beale send him?'

'I don't suppose she did,' said Lucy. 'He's with

Jackie, the girl from work. She's involved in this museum idea and she's getting involved with him.'

'Well, I don't like him,' said Giles as he turned, beaming, to accept the congratulations of an influential business acquaintance.

Lucy could not have been faulted that day. She was a splendid hostess, keeping the guests happy, seeing they were supplied with food and drink, talking and laughing and answering questions: about the wedding and the honeymoon and the home that was being prepared for them in the top floor of the big house.

Matt did not come near her and she kept well away from him, although she saw him, usually talking to somebody. For a good ten minutes it was Alys Lessing and that gave Lucy some anxious moments. She might have joined them to hear what he was telling her, but they were some distance away and she was cornered by a very boring politician, who was droning on to Giles's smiling agreement with everything he said.

Alys was smiling too, and talking while Matt listened. She didn't look as if she was hearing anything alarming, although the next time Lucy came up against her she would not have been surprised to see a tightening of Alys's lips. But Alys smiled at her fondly; whatever the topic of talk had been it had put no doubts into her mind about Lucy.

The pool filled. Lucy and a good half of the guests changed into swimsuits, oiling themselves against the hot sun. Her mother and father sat fully dressed on the terrace with long, cool drinks, a charming couple that any daughter should be proud of.

The pool was more of a social asset to the Lessings than anything else. Lucy had seen George splashing around like a walrus twice during this long, hot summer but she had never seen Alys enter the water, or even in a swimsuit; and although Giles often swam with Lucy she knew that she could have outpaced him. Today Sir George had removed his jacket, but nothing else, and Giles was for sunbathing.

Jackie and Matt were among the office set. Groups had stayed together, Lucy's friends and the Lessings' circle. Here and there the edges blurred. Laurence Gillingham was a member of the same clubs as Sir George, they and Sylvia moved in the same social strata. But the Lessings had the money and counted themselves the real aristocracy.

Lucy's friends were for the main part way down the list. This was the first time most of them had been invited to Ivory Grange and it was a good party, only needing somebody to push Lady Lessing into the deep end to make it perfect.

Jackie lay topless, face resting on folded arms, while Matt oiled her back, and Lucy wondered if he was remembering Strona. She was not. She blocked it from her mind and concentrated on massaging protective cream into Giles's shoulders. He had his father's florid complexion that freckled rather than tanned and she worked the cream well in with a practised touch.

When she put down the cream Giles reached for her bronzing lotion and she looked up to see Jackie sit up. For a petite girl Jackie was fairly busty. Alys Lessing's guests knew better than to go topless around her pool but Jackie neither knew nor cared, and she was quite capable of inviting Matt to oil front as well as back. In Alys's eyes that would be tantamount to an orgy and Lucy felt that a dip in the pool might be the easiest way to distance herself.

She said, 'I'll take a swim first,' and slipped into the water. Jackie was behaving badly. She would not have stripped off at the local swimming pool and it was

exhibitionist here; she was doing it to shock. Lucy
needed the cool water because she was feeling hot and
indignant. She swam below surface the length of the
pool, came up and over, swimming on her back in a fast
crawl, turning and retracing her course. When she saw
Matt swimming beside her she said, 'You left the lady
half done?'

It never occurred to her that she might have resented
Matt's hands stroking Jackie. She only knew that
suddenly a topless guest was funny. Even Alys Lessing
must have seen worse than that in her travels.

'You finished the feller?' said Matt.

'Absolutely.'

There were about a dozen other swimmers in the
water and around the pool it was crowded. The noise of
splashing and voices drowned what they were saying for
everyone else as they swam along together and he said
cheerfully, 'I shouldn't have thought you'd have been
worried at what Maud might be spending when all this
had landed in your lap.'

She said, 'I don't want anyone cheating her, that's all,
and I don't entirely trust you.'

'I can't think why. I'm not the one who travels under
an alias.' She raised her head then but nobody was close
enough to be listening although any number smiled and
waved when she looked around. She was not going to
make a move today that was not noticed. She went
underwater again and came up, again face to face with
Matt. He said, 'If things get too much for you when
you're walled up in your ivory tower, put a lamp in the
window and I'll climb the ivy.'

'There isn't any ivy.' Just ivory-painted walls; but she
looked up at the dark windows.

'Then put in a fire escape.'

'Some fire escape if it brought you up.' Water fell

from her hand and the diamonds flashed in the sun. She gasped, Oh, my ring! It could slip off. I shouldn't be swimming in it.'

'Surely he's got the right size by now.' But she was swimming for the side and hauling herself out.

'What was that about?' said Giles. 'What did he say that got you out of the pool like that?'

'I remembered my ring.' She clutched her hand, counting the stones. 'I shouldn't be swimming in it.'

Giles laughed. 'Well, you can't take it off today, so you'd better keep out of the water.' She towelled herself dry and he oiled her, and they joked and chatted with their guests, and when the guests started to leave everyone agreed that it had been a really lovely day.

All the clearing up would be done by the caterers and the staff. there was no tidying up by the family in the Lessing household, and Lucy and Giles and their parents went upstairs to Giles's apartment. There were easy chairs there, it was comfortable and luxurious, and a little how it might be when Lucy and Giles were married and entertaining. Although by then all the alterations would have been made.

Work was starting next week and the family—'We're all one family now' as George kept reminding them— toured the empty rooms while the future layout was described for Sylvia and Laurence.

'This will be the nursery,' Alys said, opening one door.

'*Mother!*' said Giles.

'Well, I'm not too crazy about being a grandmother,' added Sylvia.

Lucy had heard it before. She knew just how it was going to be, and as soon as things started happening of course she would be thrilled. But this evening her imagination wouldn't work. These were empty rooms, some of them used for storage, and she could not visualise them any other way.

In Giles's apartment it was easier. She made coffee there in the little kitchenette and served it. They all agreed that the party had been a great success. Lucy's parents complimented Alys, who admitted modestly that she did have a flair for that kind of thing and she thought the wedding arrangements should be getting under way.

'Oh, you're so right,' said Sylvia, breathlessly, 'and I shall need your help and advice. It would be nice to have the reception here. By then we might be in our new home, which is exactly what we want but small, of course. And Alys, George, Giles, all of you,' she gave all the Lessings a tremulous smile, 'I can't begin to tell you how thankful we are.'

They smiled away her gratitude. 'Glad to be able to help,' said Sir George.

'All in the family,' said Giles.

Everyone seemed relaxed and content, and Lucy, sitting on a footstool by Giles's chair, thought, it may be an ivory tower but there's security here and in their way everybody in this room loves me.

When her father said they should be going home Alys said, 'Not yet, surely.' But the time was right. Laurence Gillingham was too wily a social animal to outstay a welcome and Alys Lessing's protests were not meant to be taken seriously.

Lucy was sorry. She got up to go with them and whispered to Giles as they followed the others to the stairs, 'I wish I could stay.'

'So do I,' he whispered back. 'But you know how the parents are.' He meant his mother. Lucy hadn't necessarily meant in his room—there were enough spare bedrooms in the Grange—although, yes, she had meant up here, shut in safe with Giles, away from danger. 'I've a busy day tomorrow,' Giles was telling her. 'And an early start.'

'Of course.'

'Come on, Lucy,' her father called. It was like an echo from long ago when he had called to her on the landing bay at Strona. His voice had been impatient then, come *on*, child, stop dragging your heels ... but now it was bantering and indulgent.

She sat in the back of the car while her mother went over the highlights of the day and her father agreed that everything had been most satisfactory.

'That girl Jackie made a show of herself,' said Sylvia, whose own conduct had been perfect so she could sit in judgement.

'It's happening everywhere,' Lucy excused Jackie's toplessness, but her mother said primly,

'Not in public at Ivory Grange.'

'Not much, I should think, in private,' said Lucy.

'Not funny,' said Sylvia. 'And what were you talking about with the man who wants to buy Maud's cottage? We met him, he's a charmer all right. But what was he saying to you in the pool?'

She should have said they were talking about the cottage or the museum, or she couldn't remember, nothing in particular. Instead she said, 'He wants me to run away with him,' because she couldn't contain the recklessness that suddenly descended on her.

There was dead silence from the front seat. Then her father said, 'I take it you're joking.'

'Definitely not funny,' said her mother, 'and don't let anyone else hear you say anything like that.'

Nothing more was said for the rest of the journey. Their reflections in the driving mirror were glum, although when they reached the house and got out of the car Sylvia cheered up, yawning and stretching and declaring herself worn out. 'But I did enjoy myself. It's been a good day.'

Laurence had a full schedule in court tomorrow. He went straight upstairs and Sylvia soon followed. Lucy had nothing else to do but get ready for bed herself. She took off her ring and left it on the little table in the drawing-room then went into the kitchen and washed her hair at the sink. By the time she got upstairs the bathroom was empty and the doors into her parents' bedrooms were closed, no light showing round them.

She was not tired, she was restless. In Giles's apartment she had felt safe and settled, but here she was in a mess and a muddle. In her own room she sat cross-legged on the bed, fluffing her hair with a hand-drier. Half the time things seemed to be moving too fast, everything out of her control, and then too slowly. If Giles had said today, 'Let's get a special licence,' she would have said yes, and then it would have been settled for ever. She wished he had let her stay so that she would not be alone here now, but Alys Lessing would not have cared for that and although Giles laughed at his mother's old-fashioned ways he always humoured her.

But he was a kind man, a good man. Today he had told Lucy, 'I'll always be with you,' and that was what she wanted most from marriage. The Lessings were a close, united family and she wanted to be part of that.

She went down to the phone, still blow-drying her hair, and rang the Grange. Giles answered, pleased and not surprised to hear her voice. 'Just saying goodnight; and it was a lovely party.'

They talked for a few minutes and he said, 'I wish you were here.'

'I'm missing you, too. What are you doing now?'

'Nothing.'

'You wouldn't like to come round?'

'It's after midnight.' Suddenly he sounded tired. He had told her he had to make an early start in the morning and of course he didn't want to get his car out and drive all this way, especially with the chance that somebody would want to know where he was going. It was a stupid idea.

'Just a thought,' Lucy said. 'Not practical but a nice thought.' He chuckled as he realised she didn't mean it after all.

'A very nice thought. I'll see you this evening. I love you.' He added, 'There's nothing wrong, is there?'

'Now what could possibly be wrong? It was a lovely day. 'Bye, then; I love you.' She put down the phone and sat looking at it for a moment. 'I love you,' she said softly again. 'Oh, I do hope I love you.'

Upstairs she finished drying her hair and got into a cotton nightshirt. She would not try to sleep until she couldn't keep her eyes open and she was not taking sleeping pills again. She opened the library book and started to read with her radio playing softly. It was a racy read, sometimes unintentionally funny enough to give her the giggles, but the airlessness of the night made her restive and she got up to pull back the curtains.

She had kept the window shut because her light was attracting flying insects, and there was a host of moths in all sizes frantically beating against the glass. Like me, she thought wryly, daft enough to go straight for the flame. 'Believe me, gang,' she said, 'it wouldn't be worth it.' She jumped as a small pebble hit the window.

Giles, bless him, had come. She could hardly believe it. This was probably the first really rash, impetuous thing he had ever done, but he must have realised she needed him and she was touched almost to tears because he was tired and it was late and he had come.

She switched off the radio, slipped into a short white terry-towelling jacket, and tiptoed out of her room.

She had never gone to meet Giles like this before and, if he was breaking the habits of a lifetime and turning masterful and passionate, maybe he would sweep her off her feet some time and head out of town with a marriage licence in his pocket. Maybe not, but who'd have thought he would have been throwing pebbles up at her window?

She opened the front door very quietly, although she was sure no one else was awake, and called 'Hello' on a whisper. 'I'm sorry, but I'm glad you came.' Then she squawked *'You!'* in a totally different tone, because Matt was standing there.

'Had a row with Giles?'

'No.'

'Then why are you apologising? I suppose it was Giles you were expecting?'

'Why are you hanging around?'

'I want to talk to you.'

*'No.'*

'Who *are* you expecting?'

'Nobody.' She was not. She should have known Giles would not come, but if she shut this door Matt was probably going to knock on it and the best way of getting rid of him might be to let him in and to say her piece. 'A fine time to be calling,' she said, 'but all right, come in and watch you don't knock anything over.'

A crash down here would wake her parents, and after that there would be no talking but an awful lot of shouting. She closed the door after him and headed for the drawing-room. With that door shut she turned on a table-lamp beside the vase containing the last bouquet but one, hardly wilted at all.

'Who's the flower arranger?' asked Matt.

'They're from Giles.'

He looked exaggeratedly impressed. 'He gives you diamonds, he brings you flowers.

She heard herself say shortly, 'He doesn't bring them. They come from a shop and they're charged to the firm,' and she didn't know why she said that except that it was true. She demanded, 'Just what are you trying to do?'

'You shouldn't be marrying Giles Lessing.'

Why hadn't Giles come when she called him? Although if he did and found Matt here it would be the end of the world. He would not come and she should be offering up a prayer of thanks for that.

Matt stood with the light of the lamp throwing harsh shadows across his face. 'Why *are* you marrying him?'

She said savagely, 'You see yourself as God's gift, don't you?' It was obvious that he knew he could get most women; Sue and Jackie were both drooling over him. She went on, 'You expect girls to run after you and I'm a challenge, I'm the one who ran the other way. But the Strona spell hasn't travelled, so count me out.'

His eyes were unreadable. 'You haven't answered my question.'

'You asked that before and I told you before. I love him.' She was conscious of the length of bare legs and the shortness of her jacket. As she had been in a skimpy swimsuit all afternoon that was illogical but she sat down now in a little chair, holding the terry towelling at her throat and across her breasts, keeping herself hunched and huddled. He sat down, too, in a chair facing her.

'They'll stifle you,' he said, 'those I talked to today.'

'I'll survive. I want security and the cherishing that Giles gives me, and he loves me. I know what you want with me and I don't think you would do me any good.'

He almost seemed to agree. He said wryly, 'Compared

to Giles I don't have much to offer. You would be taking a chance.'

'A leap in the dark.' That phrase had always struck her as frightening. 'No, thank you. And please stay away from me.'

'Because Giles Lessing's wife must be above suspicion,' he drawled. 'Hail, Caesar!'

'Something like that.' She should not have let him into the house. 'And this isn't a good idea either. I must be losing my mind. It must be the book I'm reading.'

'What book?'

'I got it out of the library. *Passion's Price.*'

He burst out laughing. 'And what is passion's price?'

'Total exhaustion, I should think, from the way they're carrying on.' She couldn't help laughing too, and once she had started she couldn't stop. A gale of laughter swept over her and she was gasping for breath when she heard her mother call her name.

That stopped her laughing. The door into the hall was a crack ajar, the latch had not clicked, and Lucy jumped up. 'Hide,' she mouthed wildly and hurried out into the hall, this time closing the door firmly behind her.

The light was on upstairs and Sylvia stood at the top of the staircase. 'Lucy? Is that you down there?'

'Yes,' said Lucy. 'I couldn't sleep. I washed my hair and came down to get a drink and I've got the radio on.'

'I couldn't sleep either,' said Sylvia and Lucy thought, if she decides to join me I switch out the drawing-room light and get her into another room and get Matt out of the house somehow. 'I've just been to the bathroom for a couple of pills,' said her mother. 'I thought I should get to sleep at once but they should do it. And you shouldn't be wandering around at this time; you'll look a hag in the morning. I can always stay in bed.'

'Goodnight,' Lucy called and watched her mother disappear in the direction of her bedroom before she herself went back to Matt. He was standing by the little table with the lamp and the flowers where she had left her ring. He had the ring in his hand and he looked across at her and his mouth was hard. 'You're careless with your goodies,' he said.

'I'm not. I knew I'd left it there. I told you to hide. There'd have been some real hysterics if my mother had walked in on you.'

He put down the ring. 'I was spoiled for choice. I couldn't decide between the vase and the bureau. Behind the curtains never seems to work in any of the films I've seen.'

'You've got to get out of here,' she said.

'Window? Back door?'

'Better wait a few minutes.' Her mother could be looking through a window or even listening for Lucy to come upstairs. Ten minutes and the sleeping pills should be working and then she could check that the coast was clear and bundle him out somehow.

He drawled, 'So how do you suggest we pass the time?'

She heard herself say, 'Well, I'm not leaving you alone in here with the silver,' and thought she was joking. This was an idiotic game they were playing. She added 'You could sit down and tell me something about yourself.'

Maybe Aunt Maud knew more than Lucy did; he was living in her home. Of course he could spin any tale he chose, it would be easy to come up with something that could not be checked, but she sat down and waited. Matt sat down and said, as if he was giving the facts to an interviewing board, 'I spent my first ten years on a coal barge on the Grand Union Canal. I don't remember my mother. My father died when I was eleven and that's when I went up to Scotland to live with my mother's brother. He had a house on Rynish. Five years later I was on my own again, this time for good. Stop me when I start to bore you.'

'Do go on. We've reached sixteen. How old are you now? Thirties?'

'Just turned thirty, but I worry a lot.'

He was laughing at her and she asked, 'What have you been doing for the last fourteen years?'

'This and that. Taking the chances as they come.'

'Which adds up to nothing much. And you've got the nerve to come round here and tell me I shouldn't be marrying Giles.'

'You shouldn't. He'll run to fat.'

'He will not.' Giles was very like his father but it wouldn't matter, they were both nice men.

'And it's me you want,' said Matt, and those quiet words were the body blow that silenced her. Her lips curved in the shape of a smile, and she shook her head, slowly, as if someone else was turning it. When he stood up she was on her feet, too, still smiling the frozen smile, hands outflung against whatever was coming.

He took two paces towards her and she couldn't step back. Her hands had no strength to hold him off, and as he wrapped his arms around her she looked up into his face, the high cheekbones and the strong, clean mouth, and it was as if she had been waiting for him ever since Strona. Waiting and starving. She touched his mouth with her fingertips and whispered, 'This isn't fair.'

'What is?'

She had no will, no strength. She was lost in a wild abandonment of happiness so that nothing mattered beyond this. When they slipped down together she surrendered eagerly to his touch, fingers and lips caressing, and the rising urgency in her blood made a roaring in her ears.

A bell rang and went on ringing. The phone in the hall. Matt said, 'I don't believe it.'

She had to stop it. She dragged herself up, clutching at a chair for support and staggering into the hall. 'Hello,' she croaked.

'Did I wake you?' It was Giles. 'I can't get to sleep myself.' She felt weak and weird. The floor beneath her wasn't steady and she had to shake her head to clear it before she could follow what he was saying. 'Well, I have been to sleep but now I'm lying here wondering if there is anything the matter because you didn't sound yourself earlier.'

It was as though icy water had been tipped over her. She said, 'I'm all right,' and closed her eyes, shutting out everything. 'I'm sorry you were worried about me,' she said.

He said that was all right then and wished her goodnight. Lucy put down the phone and bit hard on her underlip, her head bowed until she felt Matt's hand on her shoulder. At the same time from the top of the stairs her mother started to scream . . .

# CHAPTER SEVEN

LUCY'S father arrived while her mother was still screaming. He was in pyjamas, and his greying hair, which always seemed thick and healthy, looked wispier ruffled by sleep. For the first time they both seemed old.

It was the biggest rumpus this house had ever known; compared with this her parents' rows over the years had been mild disagreements. They both set up a shrill chorus of horror as they came down the stairs. 'What's going on? What are you doing? Are you mad? How dare you? How could you?'

Matt's hand was still on her shoulder. She pushed it from her and cringed away from him because this was terrible. 'Go! Please *go*.'

The revulsion in her voice was for herself, not for him, but he didn't move and her father was shouting, 'By God, I could kill you, seducing my daughter!'

He was seducing her, but she had not been fighting. She could have stopped him but now she couldn't look at him.

'Get out,' her father roared, 'and if you ever come back here I'll blow your head off.'

You don't have a gun, Lucy thought stupidly. You'd have to borrow one. Giles has a gun. She was shaking now and her mother screeched, 'Or if you say a word about this.'

She knew that Matt was looking at her, although he answered her mother, 'You'll be glad to hear that there's nothing to tell.' Then he said, 'Lucy.' But she kept her head turned away and he said, 'Call me if you need me.'

138

She knew her father went to shove him because he said, 'I shouldn't if I were you,' in a voice that sent shivers down her spine, and then her father rushed to open the front door and slam it behind him. When they both started up again Lucy put her hands over her ears but it couldn't keep out their voices as their faces were thrust into hers.

'Did you know he was coming?' her mother mouthed through white lips.

'No.'

'But you came down and let him in.' That was her father. 'And look at you, nearly naked. What were you expecting?'

'He said he wanted to talk.' She wanted to creep away, but her father ranted on.

'What kind of fool believes that? Talk about what?'

'He doesn't want me to marry Giles.'

'And I'll tell you why.' The ruddy flush of rage was ebbing. He was beginning to look haggard and ill. 'Because he's sized Maud up, and she's got a nice little property and a decent bit of cash tucked away and he thinks you'll be coming into some of it. And this place doesn't look too bad, either. He's a fortune-hunter.'

A seducing fortune-hunter. There went one of the plots of *Passion's Price.* Although Aunt Maud's money might be a temptation to a man who took the chances as they came and who knew that he could trigger a chemical reaction in Lucy that could blow her mind.

Her mother said huskily, 'He didn't—did he?'

'I was saved by the bell.' She almost laughed and her mother slapped her face, a light stinging blow, and shrieked, 'Don't get hysterical.'

'Why not?' said Lucy, thinking, you wanted to do that and I deserved it.

'You'll keep out of his way if I have to lock you up,'

her father said. He wasn't shouting now, the blow had shocked them all.

'Go back to bed,' said Sylvia. 'You heard him, nothing happened. Come on, Lucy,' She put a trembling arm round Lucy's shoulders although she looked as if she needed supporting herself, and led her daughter back into the drawing-room. 'I'm sorry I did that,' she said, 'I was getting hysterical myself.'

She poured two brandies with shaking hands and came and sat beside Lucy on the sofa.

'Did you take those pills?' Lucy asked.

'Yes.'

'Then don't drink that.'

'Oh, the hell with it!' But Sylvia thought again with the glass at her lips and set it aside. 'He didn't——' she had to swallow twice before she could get the word out '—rape you?'

'No.' It had been a million miles from rape.

'But if the phone hadn't rung would you——'

'Yes.'

'Then we have to be sensible about this. It won't last. It never does.' Sylvia's sounded like the voice of experience, weary and sad. 'It's happened to me lots of times.' She gave a pale shadow of her enchanting smile. 'Men often make fools of themselves over me, so I can handle it. But perhaps it's never happened to you before so you're flattered and you're losing your head. I did warn you to keep away from him and tonight, that was madness. If he started talking to anyone . . . If Giles heard . . . Or his mother. It doesn't bear thinking of.' She looked scared to death.

'He won't talk,' Lucy said.

'Oh, lord, I hope not,' said Sylvia fervently. 'But you won't take that kind of risk again, will you, and you will keep away from him?'

'I'll keep away.' She felt that Matt would keep away, too. 'Call me if you need me,' he had said; if she did call she would have to be more desperate than she could imagine.

'Of course you will,' said her mother, looking longingly at the brandy glass. 'George is putting business your father's way. Your father's going through a bad patch.'

So he had been telling them for years; her mother's extravagance had always been a problem. Sylvia sighed now. 'I know I'm not much of a help but we've always managed, it's always worked out, and now you're marrying Giles it *is* going to be all right. Lucy, you *have* to marry him.'

Lucy drank her brandy, but it didn't make her feel any better and she went to bed with her self-esteem at an all-time low. She had let Giles down, she had let Matt down, and she was sorry for her parents, too. Seeing her and Matt like that must have been as harrowing for them as if she had been hauled in for robbery or discovered peddling drugs.

In a way she was an addict. This longing for Matt was an addiction. I caught a fever in Strona, she thought, and all I can do is sweat it out and one day I shall wake up cool-headed and cured. She wished she had left Strona with Matt instead of running away. She wished she could say to Giles now, 'Please take back your ring and let's just be friends again for a while because I am sick of a strange fever.'

Giles would think she was mad. Once she returned his ring it could be the last she would see of him, and she hadn't the courage to risk it.

She slept fitfully and next morning went downstairs to find her father in the kitchen. 'About last night——' she began.

'Nothing happened,' he said, which considering the performance he had given was a mighty understatement. What he meant was, 'Let's forget it,' and although there was no hope of that Lucy was prepared to pretend.

'I behaved stupidly,' she said. 'It won't happen again.'

'Good girl,' said her father. 'Bit of a misunderstanding.'

Not really, she thought. Everybody understood the situation, and this morning I understand that I have to marry Giles and be faithful to him in every way. And I will. I promise I will.

She rang Aunt Maud from a call box on her way to work because she did not want anyone overhearing her. She said, 'This time I mean it. I can't come down to you again while Matt Lomas is in your house. Do you know he came up here late last night?'

'Yes,' said Aunt Maud.

'And there was a *very* bad scene.'

'Yes.' Aunt Maud knew some of that, too. Not all of it, for sure, but she sounded subdued.

'When is he leaving?'

Aunt Maud couldn't give a date but she did offer, 'He won't be here all the time. He's going to do some buying for me.'

'Buying what?'

'Things for the museum.'

'Well, get receipts,' Lucy said shortly. 'And I'd be very happy if you'd get rid of him.'

In the office that morning they were all talking about the engagement party and what a super do it had been. 'And you're having the wedding reception there, aren't you?' said Jackie. 'What's it going to be like? They don't spare the expense. I've never had real caviare before. You will ask us all, won't you?'

'Only if you keep your jumper on,' said Kathleen.

'And the wedding reception is the bride's parents' responsibility.'

'Bet you Alys Lessing picks the menu,' said Jackie, and got no takers.

Everywhere Lucy went that day she seemed to meet people who had seen the photograph in Saturday's paper. Friends, clients, acquaintances, all said she and Giles made a handsome couple. There was some teasing and a lot of good wishes. She was working and busy but she was glad when it was time to go home and for a little while she could stop smiling and acting as if she hadn't a care in the world.

She did have cares. Life was good and would get better, but while Matthew Lomas remained within her orbit she had problems. That evening she went with Giles and her mother to see the new flat. It was about five miles away from Shady Lane, in a fantastic modern complex overlooking a bend in the River Trent. Her mother showed her round as if it was already furnished with the pieces they would bring from their old house. 'The rosewood cabinet there, and my little sofa,' and Lucy thought it was like the apartment at Ivory Grange, empty rooms that others were seeing through different eyes from hers.

The emptiness was inside her, too, although she sounded enthusiastic. 'It's going to be lovely; it will be just right for you. It was clever of you to find it.' She smiled at Giles who was holding her hand, and he smiled, too, pleased that Lucy was pleased.

She saw nothing of Matt that week. She didn't go near the Old Schoolhouse and she kept out of town as much as possible. He was still there though and his name came up.

'So what about the best man?' Jackie asked again, and now Lucy could tell her that a cousin of Giles was flying in from America with his wife. Jackie sighed. 'Just my luck. And your aunt's lodger is still playing hard to get.'

'I wouldn't have said that,' said Gail. 'You seemed to be doing all right on Sunday. You're still round at the schoolroom in the evenings, aren't you?'

Jackie was. 'Sometimes he's there and sometimes he isn't, but I can't get him to take me seriously.' She sighed again, then grinned. 'He makes you laugh, though, and somebody always finds you a job. I end up cackling like a hyena and polishing some tatty bit of brass.'

Lucy didn't talk about Matt at all. She just smiled when Jackie said, 'I suppose he isn't Miss Beale's long-lost grandson? He seems to be very well in down there,' and said,

'Of course not.'

But at the end of the third week there was no escape and she had to face him. Saturday afternoon she had a phone call at home. The voice was familiar but she couldn't pinpoint it until he said 'Bernard Beddows here,' then she asked anxiously, 'Is Aunt Maud all right?'

'Very well indeed, but I would like to see you on a matter relating to Miss Beale. Without prejudice, you understand, and strictly confidential.'

After that, of course, her car was in his drive within minutes. The door opened while her finger was still on the bellpush. He drew her in, neck stretched as he peered to left and right, and his first words were, 'I shouldn't like your aunt to know about this. Professional ethics, you understand.'

Lucy understood why he was nervous. Mr Beddows was usually a quiet gentleman, while Aunt Maud could be a very loud lady. She said, 'Yes, yes. What's going on?'

'It's this young man,' said Mr Beddows, and that was

no surprise. He led the way into his sitting-room. 'Can I offer you anything? A glass of sherry perhaps?'

'Just tell me,' Lucy begged.

'Please sit down.' So he thought she was due for a shock. 'This Matthew Lomas is a very exceptional young man.'

He paused and Lucy said, 'Agreed, but what about Aunt Maud?'

'I was her bank manager,' said Mr Beddows, 'and I am still her financial adviser.' Lucy knew all that and resisted the urge to snap 'Get *on* with it,' when he came at last straight to the point. 'But she has just withdrawn a large sum of money without consulting me. Shares that were making a good return. She won't tell me what she wants the money for and I have to say this, I think that Lomas may be persuading her to invest in some scheme of his own.'

'Is she spending it on museum exhibits?' Lucy suggested. Aunt Maud had said Matt was doing 'some buying' for her. But Mr Beddows was emphatic.

'No, we've had an excellent response. By the time we open we're going to have more than we can display.'

'How much?' said Lucy and he developed another attack of the ethics.

'I can't give you the figure but it is a considerable one, and the young man does have influence on her. You haven't been near recently, have you?' He looked at her reproachfully and produced his trump card. 'So you may not know that she is changing her will.'

Aunt Maud's will had been made when Lucy was a baby, leaving the bulk of her estate, except for personal gifts, to Lucy and her parents. Now Lucy said, 'You think she's putting Matt in?' and Mr Beddows said solemnly,

'I think, and I've heard others say it, that now you're

marrying Giles Lessing you've got no time for Maud. If she has lost you she may feel she had found a replacement?' He made that a question with raised eyebrows.

'Things aren't what they seem,' said Lucy 'but thank you for telling me what's happening. I'll go and see her and I promise I won't mention your name.'

She waited until late evening for a better chance of getting Aunt Maud alone. She should have been going out for a meal with Giles, but Mr Beddows's revelations had to be dealt with, so she pleaded another headache and felt guilty when Giles was sympathetic rather than suspicious.

In fact the headache was genuine. Things were taking a nasty turn; she was facing a grim confrontation and she wished she could take the paracetamols, go to bed and pull the sheet over her head. She did take two painkillers, but then she had to wait until ten o'clock before coming downstairs and letting herself out of the house.

Both her parents were out; if they came back before she did they would presume she was with Giles. She walked towards the town and the Old Schoolhouse with head and stomach churning.

She could not go on letting Aunt Maud be fooled like this. She had to tell her about Strona. Afterwards, of course, it was up to her what she did with her own property. Lucy didn't care about that, but she had to be told that Matt had known all about her before he knocked on her door and moved into her home.

There were lights burning in the hall and in the parlour. The schoolroom was in darkness and the street door was locked. Maud Beale opened it when Lucy knocked and her face lit up. Then she saw Lucy's expression and asked 'Are you all right? You don't look very happy.'

'Matt isn't here, is he?'

'No.' But, as Lucy breathed a sigh of relief, 'He's upstairs.'

Lucy drew her out of the hall into the parlour, glad that was empty. 'I hoped he'd be out of the house because I've got a confession to make that concerns Matt, and I should have said this weeks ago.' She spoke slowly now, feeling the weight of responsibility. 'He didn't just come down here about the cottage. He may want to buy it, I don't know about that. But when we met in here and he was supposed to be falling for me at first sight, well it wasn't the first time. We'd met before.'

'On Strona,' said Aunt Maud.

'He told you?'

'Yes.'

'And that I talked about you and that was why he fitted in so well because he knew so much about you?'

'Oh, yes,' said Aunt Maud. Of course he had told her. It would be the smart thing to do, and Matt was nothing if not smart.

The door opened and he stood there. He said, 'I thought I heard your voice,' and Lucy felt the blood draining from her face until it seemed she would faint. It was horrifying, the way nothing mattered when she was near him.

She said through tight lips, 'Listening on the landing, were you?'

'Nice to see you,' said Matt. The smile didn't reach his eyes. He stood just inside the room and Aunt Maud was leaving them, closing the door behind her. If she thought she was matchmaking she couldn't be more wrong.

Lucy snapped, 'I hear you've been managing very

nicely without me. People are saying she's lost a niece
and found a nephew.'

His sympathy was a taunting sham. 'Why, that's
terrible. I know how much it matters to you what people
say, how sensitive you are about public opinion. But,
face facts, you have dropped her since you moved into
exalted circles.'

He didn't think the Lessings were special. She flushed
more from resentment than remorse and spoke through
gritted teeth. 'I've been keeping out of your way, not
hers, although it sounds as if I should have been
watching you. Because I think you're getting money out
of her.'

'Do you now?' he drawled, eyes gleaming.

'Well it damn well looks like it,' she said furiously.
'She drew out a packet this week and nobody knows
where that's going. Do you know? *And*, surprise,
surprise, she's changing her will. Now what would you
have to do with that?' His face was inscrutable and she
almost screamed, 'Well, say something!'

He said contemptuously, 'You've got a miserable little
mind. You don't give a toss about her, just where the
money's going,' and she gasped as if she was strangling.
There was so much she wanted to say but all the words
had gone with her breath.

She turned her head and stared unseeingly into the
mirror, fighting for breath. He was denying nothing,
just lashing out at her.

'You're getting what you want with Giles, easy living,
and you're just what the Lessings want, a house-trained
bitch, hand-fed. As long as you stay to heel you should
be safe enough, but God help you if you stray. And
remember this . . .'

She saw him in the mirror—his face was a devil's—
and her eyes blurred so that for the first time everything

in the room was distorted into a green hell. She ran out of the room as he shouted, 'I could come and get you one night, you'll never be sure you're free of me,' and out of the house and through the streets and up the hill, and she didn't stop running until she was inside her own home. Even then she looked into the shadows of the hall and up towards the top of the stairs as if somewhere he might be waiting for her.

She never thought she would sleep that night. She undressed and washed and crawled into bed, still shivering. She heard the car come and the sound of her parents' voices, but she had locked the door because she couldn't face her mother peeping in to ask if she and Giles had had a good time, and she lay in darkness and over and over again she heard what Matt had said.

It was unforgivable, even if she had just accused him of being no better than a thief. Although one day when Lady Lessing was patronising her or Giles was patting her head she might just sit up and beg. She stuffed her fist in her mouth, her shoulders shaking.

He hadn't denied having the money. He hadn't denied knowing about the will. He had just turned on her, and the best form of defence was attack. Aunt Maud could have been easy pickings.

She remembered the ring. His expression when she had gone back into the drawing-room and caught him with it in his hand. If she had been a minute longer in the hall, talking to her mother, would he have pocketed it? She could not have accused him without admitting where he had been at dead of night, and when she had made that crack about not leaving him alone with the silver was it because, subconsciously, she distrusted him?

Whatever the facts, she could hardly have made a bigger mess of things. She should have kept her head and

not started hurling accusations, but that was because she
was scared of the power that Matt had over her. If he had
put his arms round her at any stage she could well have
burst into tears.

Tomorow she would be cool. She would go down
again, because of course she was not deserting Aunt
Maud now she was marrying Giles. She would ask her
about the money, and she would try to think of some
way of keeping Bernard Beddows out of it.

Right now her whole body was aching as if she had
been beaten up. She hurt all over, nerves and muscles
strained and knotted, and she did deep breathing,
relaxing from the toes up. But every time she woke in the
night she was still aching.

Next morning the headache could have started again
if she had not taken things quietly, and as soon as she
came downstairs she rang Aunt Maud. If Matt answered
she would try to salvage a little dignity. They had both
said things that would have been better unsaid. Neither
was likely to apologise, but there might be an armed
truce.

It was Maud, and Lucy said, 'It's me. I'm sorry I
dashed off like that but we had words. Did Matt tell
you?'

'He said it was time he was moving on.'

'Well, yes,' said Lucy.

'He went early this morning.'

Lucy gulped. 'Went where?'

'I don't know. But he said he won't be back.' Maud
sounded sad about that. 'I liked Matthew, I shall miss
him.'

If he had the money he might have run with it but if
the will was being changed to include him he would
surely have stayed around. Maud sighed. 'I think we've
seen the last of him.' Now it was over, and he had gone;

Lucy couldn't believe it.

She asked 'What about the cottage?'

'You didn't want me to keep it, did you?' said Maud. 'We settled that.'

'Oh!' So there was no reason to keep in touch. 'Did he tell you what the row was about?'

'No. He went upstairs and he didn't come down until they'd gone and then he said it was time he was moving on.'

Until they'd gone? Lucy croaked, 'There was nobody else there, was there?'

'Hilda Bowen and Mary Ridgway were in the kitchen,' said Maud, naming two of the biggest gossips in town. 'They came out while Matt was shouting at you.'

'They heard?' Of course they had heard ... I could come and get you one night, you'll never be free of me ...

'I'm afraid so,' said Maud.

'What did they say? What did you say?'

'Well,' said Maud, setting the scene. 'You slammed the front door behind you and Matthew went up the stairs two at a time and Mary said, "I know who he reminds me of, Laurence Olivier as Heathcliff," and Hilda said, "Was that a lovers' quarrel?" "Never," I said.'

Lucy could not have come up with anything much better herself on the spur of the moment. How could words like that be explained? 'If there had only been one of them,' Maud went on, 'I might have persuaded her she hadn't heard right. Or read the cards and warned her about lawyers and damages.'

'They'll talk, of course,' said Lucy.

'Knowing them,' said Maud, 'I expect they have.'

She had better tell her parents before anyone else did, and she found her mother still in bed, sitting up and yawning. 'I wasn't out with Giles last night,' said Lucy. 'I went to see Aunt Maud.'

'Oh, *Lucy!*' Sylvia's exasperation jerked her upright.

'Where I had a row with Matt. A shouting match.'

'I don't believe it.' Lucy had promised to keep away from that man, but a blazing row meant being involved with him.

'Believe it,' Lucy said gently. 'But he's gone now. He didn't leave an address and he isn't coming back.'

'Who says he isn't?'

'Aunt Maud.'

'Maud has a lot to answer for,' said Sylvia with real venom. 'Was there anybody else there?'

'Mary Ridgway and Hilda Bowen.' Sylvia fell back on her pillows again croaking,

'Those two old crows! Why didn't you broadcast it with loudspeakers? How are we going to explain this? What do we say?'

'Say I've got a double,' said Lucy, and her mother's howl of rage followed her out of the room.

She went walking over the hills. If she kept clear of the house until Giles was due to arrive there would be less time for recriminations, although when Giles did arrive he might have heard that yet again when she was supposed to be nursing a headache she had been in an animated encounter with Matthew Lomas.

There would have to be explanations and apologies but she did have one less worry than yesterday. Matt had gone. 'I could come and get you . . . you'll never be free of me . . .' had been anger talking. Because a threat like that was more lasting than a blow. She would remember those words long after a bruise would have faded.

Her skirt caught on a gorse bush, snagging when she dragged it loose without looking down. Suppose he turned up at the wedding, where the congregation is asked if anyone knows any just cause for stopping the ceremony, and said, 'The girl in the heirloom off-white veil married me on Strona a year ago.' She was letting her imagination run wild, but she had always known that he was capable of anything.

Supposing she said to Giles today, 'I have a demon lover who might step out of the shadows one dark night. They tell me he's gone and he won't come back, but that was why I was tearing along the high street last night; I thought he was after me.' But the quarrel she did have with Giles that day had nothing to do with Matt. The cause was much more mundane than a demon lover.

She came out of the bushes, where she had literally been hiding, as he got out of his car in front of the house. 'Let's go,' she said. They were driving down to Stratford to spend the day with business friends of the Lessings who had a boat moored on the Avon, but Giles was surprised at her eagerness to be away. He waved at her parents, watching from the window, and asked, 'Headache better?'

'Yes, thank you.'

'It's the job; you never used to have headaches. I've been telling you it's too much for you. And I'm not at all sure it's suitable, touting for advertisements, chatting up all sorts.'

Lucy tried to joke. 'We've got a very nice class of client and I like the work.'

'I've just seen your managing director,' said Giles, ignoring the interruption. 'I told him you were quitting.'

'When it's time to hand in my notice I would prefer to do it myself, thank you all the same,' she said, unnecessarily loudly.

'As long as you stay to heel you should be all right,' Matt had jeered. Giles looked at her now as if she was a tiresome puppy, scolding her with rising irritation when she refused to admit he knew best.

Lucy cancelled her notice. She did like her job but that was not her reason for hanging on to it. She might be going to need it because from Sunday her settled future suddenly looked uncertain.

On Monday night she had a call from Bernard Beddows, who was anxious to know if Maud had any inkling that he had played the mole. He had heard about the row between Matthew and Lucy. Nobody seemed to know what it was about and Maud had declared herself as puzzled as anyone. Matthew Lomas had left town, that was all Maud knew. Maud was not interested in gossip, so nobody risked it within her hearing, although it was a safe bet that the story was going the rounds and losing nothing in the telling.

'Aunt Maud doesn't know, said Lucy. 'She wasn't in the room.'

'He was very angry, I gather,' said Mr Beddows in hushed tones. 'Did he—admit anything?'

'No, he was just angry.'

She heard his slow intake of breath. 'Oh, dear, I hear he threatened you, and I fear he could be a dangerous man. But I did feel that somehow she was being taken advantage of and that you should know. She thinks a great deal of you.'

'I think a great deal of her,' said Lucy. 'And your secret's safe.' She could have added, which is more than mine is!

Jackie came into the office with a tragic face next morning announcing, 'Matt's gone. They're saying you had a row with him. What was it all about?'

'Something and nothing,' said Lucy, which was all

they were getting. Even Jackie looked into Lucy's eyes and realised that. Some thought the dangerously charming young man had had an eye on the main chance with old Maud. Some thought he had fancied his chances with Lucy, which were of course nil since she had just nailed Giles Lessing.

It made lovely gossip and by Tuesday it had reached most of Lucy's clients, so that all day she was getting either curious looks or direct questions and trying doggedly to defuse the situation. Nothing but time would do that, but she must give Giles an explanation, which she would get round to some time that evening.

He collected her from the office to take her up to his home to see two days' demolition on the new apartment, and talked all through the journey about an invitation they had for Friday night. Folk who would be there, how she should dress. He had never had any objections to the way Lucy dressed, but since Sunday he had not been quite so confident that she would always do him credit.

And his mother, waiting for them, looked even more worried than he. The gossip had reached her before him, which was unfortunate and made Lucy wish she had interrupted him and made her confession in the car.

'I've just heard a very curious thing,' said Alys. 'That on Saturday night that man who is staying at Maud's was shouting at you, saying he was coming back one night to get you. Was he drunk?'

Giles's jaw fell open, and he brought it together with a snap.

'I don't think so,' said Lucy. 'But I wasn't happy about his influence on Aunt Maud. She's been drawing out a lot of money.'

'I said that,' said Giles. 'I didn't trust him. Saturday night? That was when you went to bed with a headache and couldn't meet me.'

'It got better,' said Lucy, 'so I went to see Aunt Maud.' She saw the suspicions ticking over in his head and she couldn't blame him. Alys said sombrely, 'They are saying that he sounded like an angry man but you ran out of the house looking guilty.'

This time Giles's jaw fell open and stayed open. 'There has been no kind of . . .' Alys Lessing gave a little dry cough, clearing her throat '. . . no encouragement offered by you to this young man? You gave him no reason to think you could be . . .' another cough, although she could hardly have been putting this more gently '. . . interested in him?'

'Of course not.' Giles snorted, and his mother turned to him with a sad, sweet smile.

'Some women don't seem to realise when they are being provocative, my dear. Still, I hear that the man has left town and is not returning.'

Lucy said nothing and Alys went on. 'I have never been one to interfere, but I do find it distasteful hearing that someone who is practically one of the family has been involved in a public brawl.'

Mary and Hilda were all the public any brawl would need, and then Lucy had hared up the Saturday-night high street, generally recognisable as Giles Lessing's bride-to-be. She began to say, 'I'm sorry——' until Alys sighed.

'Of course, you are your mother's daughter.'

Then Lucy snapped, 'That's fairly certain and there's not much we can do about it,' and disapproval settled over Lady Lessing like a black hooded cape from which her furious face glared.

She'll never like me or trust me again, thought Lucy, and although it didn't really matter she said, 'I'm sorry.'

But Alys could not bring herself to speak and Giles went ahead silently up to his apartment. When they got there he said, 'You've upset mother.' She certainly had and she had upset him, too; she said again, 'Sorry.'

'Do you think he's been getting money out of Miss Beale?'

'Honestly, I don't know.'

'And that was what the argument was about?'

That was how it had started but she could hardly tell him what Matt had said. She said, 'He's a forceful character. The discussion got out of hand, and I've got a quick temper myself.'

'You have?' Giles was surprised to hear it, and it was another cause for concern. It alarmed him and afterwards she thought that he often looked at her speculatively, waiting, she supposed, for the next outburst.

Four weeks passed, a long slow month. The history society's enthusiasm for their little museum was unabated. Aunt Maud was enjoying that, and although the others talked about Matt, missing his energy and charisma, wondering what he was up to now, Aunt Maud never mentioned him.

The gossip was dying down, with nothing to refuel it, although when Lucy called at the Old Schoolhouse she was sometimes asked if she had heard from him. She said, 'No, why should I?' and nobody told her why because there was something unapproachable about Lucy these days, even when she was smiling.

Her parents sensed it. Neither of them had ever been perceptive about Lucy's emotions but now they had stopped harassing her. They refused to listen to the gossip. Giles was still phoning and fetching Lucy, the flowers were still coming and she was still wearing his ring. Sylvia told herself and everyone else that everything was fine, and Laurence looked haggard and hoped to God it was.

Lucy took each day as it came, because for the present

that was how life had to be lived. But when Giles
collected her from the Gables that Saturday afternoon to
take her up to Ivory Grange to see how their future
home was progressing she thought, what a charade this
is. We both know we're never going to live together here
or anywhere else. In her heart she supposed she had
always known that and in the last month the Lessings
had shown it, too.

Lady Lessing had avoided Lucy wherever possible
and been distinctly chilly during their brief meetings.
Sir George seemed to be trying to keep out of it. She only
saw him twice in that month and both times he was gruff
and embarrassed, exchanging a few words and clearing
off rapidly. Giles appeared to be in a constant state of
anxiety and Lucy felt sorry for them all.

Poor Giles was realising that yet again he had not
found Miss Right and very soon he was going to suggest
they should both be having second thoughts. So far as
Lucy was concerned the engagement was over, but he
had been kind to her and she wanted to leave him his
pride. He would take a jilting far harder than she would,
and for her parents' sake she did not want to make
enemies of the Lessings. If it could end without
bitterness, that would be salvaging something from a
relationship that was doomed. And once Giles had set
her free she would begin to live her life.

The air in his apartment tasted of dust. He was not
sleeping up here any more but he was still using the
living-room and he poured stiff drinks as soon as they
got in. 'Just finished your last week,' he said.

Lucy put her drink down. For a moment she thought
she was being handed her notice as the future Mrs
Lessing, but he was talking about work and she said,
'Well, no, I'm not leaving.'

Giles sighed deeply and drank deeply. 'You've

changed,' he said. 'You're not the girl I used to know, but I'm still prepared to marry you,' and she couldn't check a drawling, 'Gee, thanks,' that brought a flush to Giles's face. But he drained the glass and said hoarsely, 'You're beautiful.'

They had rarely been alone together this month. Little beads of sweat were breaking out on his upper lip and forehead and he was suddenly on top of her in the armchair where she sat. She stiffened in a reflex of revulsion, shoving with fists and knees, and he got up as quickly as he had flopped down and blustered, 'You've got to get yourself together, my girl.'

She was together; he was the one stammering and falling about. 'You should count yourself lucky I will marry you with your family.' He was being too pompous for words and she asked with mock concern,

'Now would that be my mother or Aunt Maud who's offending your sensibilities?'

'Oh, them,' Giles sneered. 'They're the least of your drawbacks. I'm talking about your old man and the fraud squad.'

Suddenly it was deadly serious. She could hardly get out the words, 'What do you mean?' and Giles muttered about ways and means of getting the gen, and needing to investigate before Lessing Electronics with their reputation could get involved. And learning about something that sailed very close to misappropriation of funds.

She could believe it. That kind of thing did happen. Her father did have business worries and not many scruples. She was appalled but not really surprised, and although she couldn't marry Giles she was touched that he was prepared to stand by her if these kind of rumours were circulating.

He said, 'As we're buying the property, that should give him a chance. But if it did come out he could end up in prison and then you'd have to finish with them.'

He meant, disown them if a scandal broke, but she could not see Alys Lessing accepting the daughter of a man who was skirting bankruptcy, and worse. 'What does your mother say?' she asked.

'She doesn't know. We'll keep it from her if we can.' Lucy gripped her fingers together and said shakily,

'I don't think I could face waiting for your mother to find out my father's a swindler. Charlotte Machin said you want Snow White up here, but if you brought her home your mother would ask some funny questions about those dwarfs.'

'That's crazy talk,' said Giles as she took off the ring and put it carefully on the arm of the chair.

'You'd better have this back,' she said and she saw the relief in his eyes.

He didn't follow her. He had seized the chance of escape she offered, and as she closed the door he almost collapsed into the chair. It was the heat and the dust up here that were making him feel sick, he told himself, and not because he was ashamed of the way he had failed Lucy.

Lucy walked about a mile before a Land Rover, with a farmer she knew at the wheel, picked her up. He was a large, kindly, incurious man, and saw nothing peculiar in Lucy Gillingham taking a walk. He discussed the weather with her and the state of the crops and dropped her on the outskirts of Edgeford. She went to the Old Schoolhouse.

There were people there but she said, 'I must talk to you,' and Aunt Maud got up. Bernard Beddows watched anxiously.

Perhaps Maud Beale was expecting something like this because she went upstairs to her bedroom, one of the few places where nobody would disturb them, and waited until they were inside with the door closed before she asked, 'What about?'

Lucy held out her ringless hand and Maud gasped, 'You haven't lost your ring?'

'I gave it back. Now I've got to tell my mother and father and that's going to be one of the worst moments of my life. They'll be in a terrible state. I'm not sure now that Sir George will buy the house, and Giles has just told me how desperately we need the money.'

Maud was not surprised. Even when Lucy told her, 'He says the fraud squad could be in,' she only said,

'I wish I could do more. I suppose I could sell the house.'

Lucy flung her arms around her. '*No!*' But she wondered what Aunt Maud had done already and asked, 'Did you let him have some money the week before Matt left?'

'Nobody's got to know about that. Bernard, was it?' She didn't wait for an answer. 'But there was no sense in Laurence waiting until I was dead when he needed it now.

'I thought you might have given it to Matt,' Lucy said. That astounded Aunt Maud.

'*What?*' You didn't say anything like that to Matthew, did you? That wasn't why he upped and went?'

'What did you think the reason was?'

'Because he didn't want you to marry Giles.'

'Why didn't he say he wasn't getting money from you?' Lucy wailed. 'That was all he needed to do. I'd have believed him.'

'Didn't see why he needed to, I suppose,' said Aunt Maud. 'Well, it wasn't a very nice way to be carrying on, was it? Accusing him like that.'

'Nor was the way he carried on,' said Lucy. 'Do you have any idea where he went?'

When she was free of Giles she had always planned to find Matt again, even if it meant going back to Strona and camping out on the cottage doorstep, but Aunt Maud said, 'I've got his address on Rynish somewhere. I think there's a phone number.'

Joy hit her first, and then panic. She turned the keeper round on her finger and kept her eyes on it and said in a small voice, 'You wouldn't ring him for me, would you? I've got to go home now and tell my mother and father. I've got to keep calm, but if I hear Matt's voice I could crack up.'

She raised wide eyes in a white face and Aunt Maud said, 'He might not be there, but what message?'

He might not come. He had had no time at all for her when he left. She said, 'Just that I'd like to see him, and that I need him. He did once say he'd come if I needed him.'

# CHAPTER EIGHT

LUCY needed somebody on her side during the hours that followed. When she got home her father was in his study and her mother was dressed for an evening at the theatre, looking ethereal in misty blue.

Sylvia had always been slim, but now Lucy realised she was thinner than ever, and there was apprehension in her face when she turned to look at Lucy walking into the drawing-room. She had obviously felt the strain of recent weeks, too.

'I can't marry him,' said Lucy, 'and he doesn't want to marry me.'

'Why?' her mother whispered and she had to be told the truth.

'We were wrong for each other, and he didn't like the looks of Father's books when they did a spot of espionage.'

'What are you talking about?' Sylvia pushed past her, running towards the study door. Lucy stared at a flower display, and hoped that Giles would remember to cancel them, until they came back into the room together.

Her father said heavily, 'You've let us down.'

'How bad is it?' Lucy asked. 'Giles was talking about the fraud squad.'

'Good lord, no. Some speculation that didn't work out. Nothing I couldn't have handled, given time and the breaks.' He sounded calm, almost offhand, but his face was grey.

'How far did Aunt Maud's money go?'

'It helped, getting my share of the will in advance; her heart's in the right place, old Maud's. The money for this would have got us clear. I thought George was dragging his heels. Are they still going through with the sale?'

'I don't know,' Lucy admitted and Laurence said with weary cynicism,

'Pity you couldn't have kept Giles happy a bit longer.'

'And cheated him as well?' said Lucy.

The doorbell rung, startling them all like a pistol shot. Sylvia whimpered, 'They've come for me. I can't face anybody.'

'I'll tell them,' said Laurence and Sylvia cowered on the couch, her face in her hands, while Lucy stood helplessly by until her father came back.

'I told them you were off colour,' he said, and in the same flat voice to Lucy, 'I did it for you, you know. For your mother and you.'

He had done it for himself, too; he enjoyed the good life as much as anyone. Lucy had never cost him much. Sylvia sobbed and it was his wife he went to, sitting down beside her, putting an arm around her. Lucy said, 'Aunt Maud offered to sell her house for you.'

Sylvia went on crying and Laurence said, 'We couldn't let her do that,' but Lucy thought, you might, even though it might kill her.

At last her mother said hesitantly, 'I suppose you couldn't try again? Go back and tell Giles you——'

'No,' said Lucy. 'For the very good reason that I couldn't bear him to touch me.'

She went to her room alone and left them together. She did not know what plans they were making, but was very much afraid that they were counting on Aunt Maud's house. If there was evidence of wrong practice it would not be long before everyone who had invested through her father's firm would be clamouring for their cash. She couldn't see what she could do or what the future held. She was heartsick and weary, only certain of one thing. She knew with crystal clarity that she loved Matt and would continue to love him through all the days and nights of her life.

Sunday was a strange day. Her father ate no breakfast and left early, and she wondered if he would be calling at the Old Schoolhouse. Every time the phone rang she held her breath, but it was never news of Matt, and she answered calls for her mother with the excuse that she was unwell.

Sylvia stayed in bed, heavy-eyed from sleeping pills and looking genuinely ill; and Lucy answered calls for herself—there was of course nothing from Giles—by pretending that everything was as usual. Tomorrow everyone would know but today she told nobody anything.

Even the old house itself seemed to reproach her. It was in disarray because Sylvia had been selecting what she was keeping. The rejects were marked with chalk crosses and Lucy began polishing them. There would still have to be a sale; maybe they would fetch more if they looked good, and she had to do something.

She prepared no meals. She couldn't have eaten and her mother wanted no food. Sylvia sipped a little orange juice, and there was nothing that Lucy could say to cheer her up. When Lucy said anything she turned her head away.

Her father's car returned when dusk was beginning to fall. As the shadows lengthened Lucy had begun to wonder if they would ever see him again. Absconding was no more incredible than embezzling. Perhaps he had left them to face the music. She would need all her strength for that, because her mother would certainly go to pieces. Or run off with the first eligible man who offered.

Lucy had gone into the kitchen, made herself a cheese sandwich, and was sitting on the edge of the table forcing herself to swallow it. Trying to keep up her strength with a cheese sandwich was pretty pathetic, but if he did not come back tonight she must not have a swimming head because she had starved herself all day.

She was gulping down a mouthful when she heard his car and she was still in the kitchen when he walked in. He moved like a man in shock. 'He's down there,' he said. 'Matthew Lomas. At Maud's.'

She raced out of the house. She heard him call, 'Lucy!' but she had gone. She couldn't wait to get out her car and she dared not drive anyway. Her head was swimming now and she was shaking like a leaf but all that mattered was that Matt had come, so from now on nothing was too terrible to face.

She ran through the town again, and she was glad the door was shut because that should mean that all the history society were not flocking in. Aunt Maud opened the door, just a little at first, then wide enough to let Lucy through. She was grinning like the Cheshire cat. 'We're keeping it dark,' she said gleefully. 'We don't want company yet. He's in the parlour; I'll just get a cup of tea.'

She went down the hall, and Lucy opened the parlour door and saw a stranger. It was Matt, but in suit, collar and tie, he looked different. 'You came,' she said.

'I told you to call me if you needed me.' He sounded as if this was some sort of business meeting. She put a hand out but he moved no nearer, and her hand fell to her side because this was not Matt at all.

'Why did you come?' she said.

'To put things right.' The only way he could put things right was by being Matt again. They had parted in anger and she could have taken up from there but how could she plead with a stranger?

'How?' she said.

He sounded weary. 'You should know, if anyone does.

With money, my mercenary little love.' His eyes were as hard as the rocks of Strona. 'Have you talked to your father?'

'He just—said you were here.'

'I've made him an offer for the Gables, subject to contract. I'll probably turn it into apartments or a small hotel.'

Put things right with money, he had just said. She asked, 'Do you have the capital?' and thought that he probably had. He opened the door and called,

'Maud, you have told her?'

Aunt Maud's voice came clearly. 'Told her what?'

'That I've got the money?'

'Matthew's a very successful man,' Aunt Maud called back. 'And I've done his horoscope and the sky's the limit. The tea's nearly ready.'

'I can produce more down-to-earth figures,' said Matt.

'Why didn't you tell me?' Lucy asked.

She didn't *care*, but why all the secrecy? She felt as if she had run a long, hard race and finished last. She sat in the nearest chair and he sat by the window. It was getting dark, it was time the lights were on.

He said, 'I never said I was a loser. I make a very good living, and in another ten years I'll have healthier balance sheets than the Lessings. But I didn't want it to matter that much. I had a crazy idea that some time, when I said "Come with me", you would, without counting the cost.

'By the way, how did it end between you and Giles? Was it because your father's firm's in difficulties?'

She could not tell this man with the lean, hard face, 'It ended for me because I am in love with you,' so she shrugged and said 'What with this and that Giles went off me. But yes, the idea of a scandal really scared him. Why are *you* helping us?'

It must be because he felt something for her, but he said, 'I shouldn't like to see old Maud sold up. I've always had a soft spot for her.' And, in answer to Lucy's puzzled look, 'Since last May. I followed you down here when you left Strona and called on Maud. We talked about you and left it that if you ever mentioned me to her she should give you my address. You didn't, but Maud and I kept in touch.'

'She knew about the ring of rock?'

'She knew we'd met on Strona.' He grinned. 'That might not have been the genuine ring. Nobody knows for sure, but it's my guess and I've been in every cave on Strona. I've been taking a boat out there ever since I went to Rynish when my father died.'

He crossed long legs, sounding as though he was making small talk while they waited for the tea tray.

'The house was my uncle's. He was a recluse and a scholar, and he taught me a lot. The old family house was turning into a ruin, but I kept it standing. After he died I borrowed and went on working, and now,' his grin was cynical, 'it's my home and my headquarters and almost as impressive as Ivory Grange.'

She said, 'Marvellous,' and it was, although she should have known that the confidence he generated was justified. Of course he was no loser. 'No wonder you could help get a poxy little museum off the ground. You were playing games. And with me.'

'Not entirely,' he said. 'I wanted you from the moment I first set eyes on you. The ring of rock might be phoney but the lust was real.'

She didn't need anyone to tell her that, but with her it was love and she said quietly, 'It must have been. It brought you down here.'

'That it did,' he admitted, and laughed at himself. 'I must be very conceited, because there were times when I thought I could outbid Giles without mentioning hard cash.'

Even now she couldn't say the money didn't matter. It didn't to her, but without it her father would go to jail and Aunt Maud might lose her home. She tried to smile. 'My father looked like he'd had the shock of his life. Worse than last night when I told him Giles and Sir George knew he'd been fleecing the customers. I suppose he was prepared for that, but he never expected to get an offer from you and it will be the kiss of life to my mother. Thank you. I hope I'll be able to repay you some time.'

If he would touch her the right words would come, but he made no move and she said with what she felt was pathetic provocation, 'Am I part of the bargain?'

'No, thank you,' he said cheerfully.

'That's a relief; I wasn't sure about that. Are you staying?' She almost sounded amused.

'For a few days.'

'How do you manage to take time off from work?'

'I don't.' Perhaps he had for a while on Strona, although most of the week he could have been commuting to the mainland; and from here there was fast transport anywhere if you could pay.

'My father would be very impressed by the suit. Nobody round here is going to recognise you.' Her words sounded to her like pebbles rattling in a tin can. 'You'll be wanting to look the house over, of course.'

'Of course.'

'I hope you don't find anything hidden that makes it good for nothing.'

'That can happen,' he said grimly and she wondered if he meant her with her 'mean little mind'.

She jumped up to switch on the lights as Aunt Maud came in carrying the tray. 'All our troubles are over,' she said with enforced gaiety,' 'so long as we don't have death-watch beetle in the Gables. It could make a nice little hotel. You must recommend it to the folk who visit the museum.'

She must shut up. She was sounding a bigger fool by the minute. She wanted to get away, but not back home where they would be reminding her that Matt had been attracted to her so maybe she could still end up with a rich man.

She said, 'I've had a grim day and I don't much want to go back. Could I have my little room tonight?'

Over the years Lucy had stayed occasional nights here and now Aunt Maud said, 'Of course you can. You know it's always ready for you. Well,' she amended, 'I've only got to get the sheets out and I'll do it right now. Pour yourselves some tea.'

Lucy lifted the pot, which seemed heavier than usual, and Matt said, 'You wouldn't be staying because I'm here?'

'No.' It was all she could do to keep the pot steady. She poured a stream of amber liquid very carefully into a cup, biting her lip with concentration and to stop it trembling.

'The house is the only deal you're getting.'

'Don't worry,' she said. 'Nothing else is on offer. Pour yourself some tea.' She took her cup without bothering with milk, lemon or sugar, and went upstairs after Aunt Maud, into the little room where she had sometimes cried herself to sleep as a child.

Maud was starting to make the bed and Lucy went round the other side, tucking in the sheets. When they reached the white quilt Maud said, 'Matthew said you hadn't wanted him to know who you were on Strona and you never mentioned him at all when you came back, so I couldn't very well say he'd been here, could I?' Lucy shook her head and Maud made a show of getting the quilt just right. 'I spoke to him on the phone once or twice and he always asked me how you were, and I sent him that photograph out of the magazine and told him you and Giles were probably getting married.

'He did want to buy the cottage, I did sell it to him, but I think you were what brought him down here. Right away he wasn't sure that Giles was the man for you.' Maud was facing it out now, looking Lucy in the eye, and nodding to show her own agreement with everything she was saying. 'And I was never all that sure about Giles myself, although everybody else kept saying what a good match it was for you.' She gave the bedding a final pat.

'Anyhow, everything's working out for the best. You've handed Giles his ring back and Matthew's here. Third visit, third time lucky.'

'Put it another way,' said Lucy. 'Giles took his ring back and Matt turns out to be loaded, but I don't think he sees himself as a consolation prize.' She smiled widely. 'And I like being free again, so please don't interfere any more.'

Aunt Maud must stop kidding herself that Matt had come back to claim Lucy. 'We're just friends,' Lucy said tritely. 'I didn't get much sleep last night and I've been on tenterhooks all day, so would you mind if I had a very early night?'

The little room seemed a bolt-hole where she could shut the door and curl up and sleep. She needed sleep, and Aunt Maud fussed for a while then went downstairs and left her alone. She had a few belongings here, a nightshirt in one of the dressing-table drawers, some make-up in another drawer. She went to the bathroom, undressed and washed.

Matt was here. Ruin and disgrace no longer threatened, and when she was rested she would appreciate what a relief that was. But now the only thing on her mind was that Matt was here. She loved him, belonged to him; some time the guard of his pride must slip so that she would be able to reach and touch him.

She could hear the undertone of voices below. There must be visitors in the house now; it would be all over town tomorow that Matt was back. She thought of the witchy mirror in the green room and almost believed she could draw an enchantment around her that would bring him to her.

She slept and in her dreams she must have done that because she woke in the night and stretched out a hand for him. I dreamed I was on Strona, she thought, head thrown back on the pillow, tears sliding down her cheeks.

It had to be late. There was no sound of voices now, and through the window the stars were thick in the sky. It felt like the dead of night, and, when she switched on the little bedside lamp long enough to check her watch, she saw that it was.

Matt was here. She had often felt his presence. Perhaps she carried him with her, in her heart and her mind, but now it was a physical fact. He was under this roof, just along the corridor, and she wondered if he was awake.

If he was, perhaps he was thinking of her. She sat up, clasping her hands around her knees, hair falling around her face, as she tried with fierce intensity to work the spell, every nerve in her calling to him.

She watched the door and willed it to open. She imagined herself slipping out of her body, floating the little way to his room, standing beside his bed and beckoning.

'Come,' she whispered, but nothing happened; telepathic signals were plainly not going to work. She was no great shakes as a witch, but she didn't lie down again; she couldn't have slept. This is stupid, she thought. The magic's still there, it *is*, and we should not be apart when we could be together with no more misunderstandings.

Heart thumping, she came out of her room into the silent house. Not that a house as old as this was ever silent. There were always creakings and rustlings as though the house stirred in its sleep. Her eyes were used to the dark and she made her way carefully along the carpeted corridor, dodging the squeaking boards.

She passed the next door to her room and reached Matt's door. Aunt Maud's room was down at the end of the bathroom.

Suddenly it was surprisingly cold, so that she shuddered in her cotton nightshirt and felt her skin go clammy. The house didn't have cold spots; this chill was inside her, and as she reached the door she knew that she was scared. She was sure she attracted him still. To her it was an overpowering natural force but if he was determined to resist it she had no doubt that he could.

It was one thing to be refused when you could pretend to shrug it off with a smile, but if she went to his bed and he sent her away that would be horrendous. She had to be more subtle than this. He was staying for a few days; in that time she could surely find some way to win him back, but she couldn't offer herself naked and defenceless.

Her fingers had stiffened on the latch and she drew her hand away, stepping on to a floorboard that creaked. She froze for a moment. The door opened and Matt looked out.

When she jumped back he glared. There was no other word for it. If she had been inside his room and he had looked at her like this she would have shrivelled up. 'I hope you weren't calling on me,' he said.

She had just decided that would be self-destruction. She said, 'Have you forgotten? The bathroom's at the end of the passage,' and she walked on and got into the bathroom before the shakes got her.

He would have turned her out. She would have felt even worse after that, and heaven knew she felt wretched enough now.

Rejection hurt with a searing pain, that she had rejected Matt, more than once, so maybe he had ended up hating her. She had not been prepared to give up anything for him when he seemed to have nothing but himself to offer, and now she knew he was a man of property she was eager and loving. That was how it seemed, and it did not look good. She did not know how she was going to prove that she was not a gold-digger and never had been. She did not know if he would ever believe that she would have lived with him in the cottage on Strona, and fished for food, and grown vegetables on a seaweed bed.

She ran back to her own room and the boards creaked beneath her feet. If he had heard that creaking board outside his door he could not have been sleeping soundly. But that was small comfort. She was not fooling herself now that he would have been thinking of her . . .

Aunt Maud and Matt were in the kitchen when Lucy came down. She had heard them and stayed upstairs until the last minute so that she could dash down, gulp a cup of coffee and run. She had quite a day ahead of her, and sitting at a breakfast table listening to Aunt Maud and looking at Matt was no way to steady her nerves.

She would be back this evening and pray that things would be easier then. She lied, 'I overslept. What are your plans for today?'

'I'm going up to your house,' said Matt.

She crossed her fingers ostentatiously. 'I'll hear how that goes after work.' She would have to go home tonight; she was not sure she wanted to sleep here any more.

'We had a millstone delivered yesterday,' said Aunt

Maud, spreading honey on her toast. Lucy's eyebrows shot up.

'What?' A thunderbolt yes, a bolt from the blue, but a *millstone*?

'There used to be a windmill by Crocketts' farm,' Aunt Maud explained. 'It burnt down over seventy years ago but they've given us one of the millstones.'

'Fancy. Lovely,' said Lucy. 'A millstone.' She drained her coffee cup. 'Have you seen all the stuff that's come in since you were here? We haven't been idle in your absence.'

When she looked at Matt she wanted to say, 'Smile at me, touch me,' but his eyes never softened so she said, 'Bye, love,' to Aunt Maud and kissed her cheek, and over Aunt Maud's head she said, 'Goodbye,' to Matt, thinking, I said goodbye to you the night my father ordered you out and I told you to go. Matt never came back; what shall I do if he never does?

She had to go home for her car before she went to work. The house doors were open and she scooped up her handbag and keys and called, 'It's only me and I'm going to be late for work. I'll see you this evening.'

Her father, fully dressed and looking anxious, came down the hall from the kitchen.

'It was a genuine offer,' she said, 'and he does have the money. He'll be up here today. I must go.'

She got her car out of the garage and drove it to her usual parking spot, and ran up the stairs into the office. They were all there, discussing what they had done over the weekend. Lucy dodged questions and listened to Gail's account of fitting a new fridge in her kitchen. Then work started.

It was almost half an hour before Jackie noticed that Lucy was not wearing her ring. Jackie and Lucy were at their table, looking over the sheets for next Saturday's paper, when Jackie whispered, 'Where's your ring?' as if this might be some distressing secret.

Phones were ringing so that nobody else overheard and Lucy said, 'It's off.'

'Not the wedding?' Obviously the ring was.

'That, too,' said Lucy.

'Oh, I'm sorry.' Jackie's face puckered with pity. 'Why?'

'Irreconcilable differences,' Lucy intoned.

She didn't look heartbroken and Jackie tried a little joke. 'Like his mother?'

'That was about fourth on the list,' said Lucy, and Jackie was almost sure she was not putting on a brave face. 'And talking of relations,' Lucy said, 'Matt's back at Aunt Maud's.'

Jackie's expression of delight changed almost immediately into a knowing leer. 'So, you break off your engagement and Matt's back! I'll bet he was top of the list.' Lucy shook her head but Jackie went on, 'So that's why I never made any headway. I always thought there must be somebody else, *and* I thought it might be you.'

'Don't bet on it,' said Lucy. 'He's doing a property deal down here.'

'Doing what?' Jackie's head was bowed and close to Lucy's; both girls seemed to be considering the mock-up papers.

'He could be buying our house and turning it into a small hotel or apartments.'

'Don't tell me he's got money as well? Oh, well, I suppose this means Giles is on the market again, too.'

'So far as I'm concerned.'

Jackie grinned. 'If I get in quick I might catch him on the rebound. Although any girl in her right mind would fancy Matt more, even without the money.' She cackled with laughter and Kathleen called down the room,

'What's the joke?'

'You'll never credit it,' Jackie chortled, 'but we're

laughing because Lucy has given Giles his ring back.'

The others didn't laugh; their faces were shocked and sympathetic. But there had been rumours, and when Jackie went on to explain that Matt Lomas was back in Edgeford and probably buying the Gillingham house, then they believed that Lucy had handed back the ring rather than that Giles had jilted her.

Jackie teased, 'How about another picture this week? "Our ad-girl with tycoon two?"'

Kathleen was horrified. '*Jackie!*'

It was a poor-taste joke and Lucy cringed, but in public she had to keep smiling.

On Mondays she went the rounds of her usual clients. Nobody noticed that her ring had gone, but a few asked, 'How's Giles?' and then she had to say, 'I'm sure he's fine but we've decided we're not getting married. 'Then they said they were sorry and she said, 'Don't be.'

She didn't go back into Edgeford for her lunch hour. Instead she bought a salad bap and a carton of milk in one of the villages, and parked off a road overlooking the hills. When she was quiet like this she knew that there was more than a chance that Matt would go away and never say, 'Come with me,' again and her eyes misted, beginning to sting.

She fished for a tissue and blotted her lashes and ate her lunch, thinking, I shall follow him. Somehow I shall think of a way to follow him.

Her parents were home when she arrived there after work and they both seemed to be in a daze.

'He likes it,' said her father slowly. 'His surveyors are coming tomorrow but I don't think any major flaw would have got past him. He went all over. I shouldn't think he misses much.'

'I'm sure he knows a weak spot when he sees one,' said Lucy.

Her mother was dressed and made up and pretty

again; she even had a meal ready. Lucy went upstairs
and changed out of yesterday's clothes into a pink linen
button-through dress and a linen jacket in the same
shade. They sat round the table in the little dining-room.
The sideboard carried a chalk cross but the table and
chairs had been scheduled for moving with them. They
ate a quiche that Lucy had cooked and put in the freezer
and that Sylvia had defrosted and heated up.

Subject to tomorrow's verdict Matt would like them
out as soon as possible, which couldn't have suited them
better. The new apartment was unlikely now but there
should be enough left over to find somewhere, and in the
meantime they could stay with friends. Aunt Maud
would always have Lucy.

When she said 'Maud', Sylvia sounded quite sentimental because it had not been a charming layabout that
Aunt Maud had introduced to Lucy; it had been a
charmer with excellent prospects.

'He arrived at Maud's while I was there,' Laurence
told Lucy. 'Maud was— well, we were both upset.'

'He's doing it for you, isn't he?' said Sylvia, smiling
her misty smile.

'He won't lose on it,' said Lucy. 'He doesn't lose. And
if he's doing it for anyone else it's for Aunt Maud. He's
fond of her. He didn't want her to be sold up. He told
me.'

'That's sweet of him,' said Sylvia. 'But of course this
does make all the difference.'

To everything, thought Lucy. We're saved and that
makes a change. But now Matt's plans do not include
me, and that is a terrible difference.

'He couldn't wait,' said her mother. 'But I said of
course you'd be going down to Aunt Maud's this
evening.'

'Of course,' Lucy murmured.

Things were humming again in the Old Schoolhouse.

They had come along to say hello to Matt, but they had heard that Lucy had broken with Giles Lessing and that was another reason for coming. To ask Maud, or to see for themselves, just what was going on.

When Lucy walked in all the faces swivelled towards her and curiosity seemed as thick as fog in the air. It must have looked to them as though Lucy and Matt were glad to see each other. He was standing at a table by one of the windows, going through some old posters he had not seen until now, and when she came into the room he called, 'Come and look at this.'

She went to him, smiling, and he held the curling yellowing poster flat on the table. It was an advertisement for bicycles, featuring a simpering lady in long skirts and leg-o-mutton sleeves and a muscular young man with a waxed moustache. 'Bicycle for Strength and Beauty' it read and Lucy said, 'I like it.'

'She looks a strong girl, doesn't she?' said Matt.

'And isn't he a beauty?'

They carried on like that, seemingly together, but Lucy knew there was an unbridgeable void between them. She went out to see the millstone propped up against a tree and so covered with green moss that it could have been part of the lawn, and declared it looked fine where it was and she couldn't see why they couldn't leave it there. Matt agreed with her.

'Things went all right today?' she asked him. 'My father seemed hopeful.'

'I think so. It's quite a sound property.'

They were talking quietly. They walked away from the millstone, and she said, 'They'd love to be out by the end of the week. Can things move that fast?'

'Yes.' They were watched, walking and talking, and knowing nods were exchanged by Aunt Maud's cronies.

When the others went home, so did Lucy. She said she would be down tomorrow and Matt said he might see her then, but it meant nothing at all. They were completely apart from each other and if she tried to get closer she knew that he would handle her in the way he had dealt with Jackie, refusing to take her seriously and leaving her with no hope at all.

Matt was not around after all on Tuesday night. 'Business,' Aunt Maud explained. By Wednesday night everyone knew that he was buying the Gillingham house, and Bernard Beddows was the only one who was worried.

There were fewer of the history society there on Wednesday evening, only those who actually had a job to do. Matt was helping to put up some shelves and Lucy was cutting sandwiches in the kitchen when Bernard came in, did a quick check that the room contained nobody else, and asked in low urgent tones, 'Is Maud buying your house?'

'Matt is,' said Lucy, 'and not with her money. He owns property and a flourishing business.' Bernard had been so concerned for his old friend that she had to put his mind at rest. 'She gave that money to my father; it was his share of her will. That was why she was changing it.' And Bernard Beddows said that that was all right then, because it was staying in the family.

He liked Matt, and he was relieved that his suspicions were unfounded. Now it seemed that Lucy and Matthew were getting together and he added archly 'Although Matthew might be family before long.' But when Lucy looked at him he felt that he must be getting old, because he seemed to be blundering from one gaffe to another ...

Lucy was the only one sleeping in the house in Shady Lane that week. Her parents were with friends and, although there was Lucy's room at Aunt Maud's, she said she preferred to stay the week out in her own bedroom. Nights were bad enough as it was, full of regrets and longings, without knowing that Matt was only a minute away. More than once, in the small hours, she might have gone to him and said, 'I would not have married Giles and I was coming to look for you before I knew you had anything but the clothes you stood up in. Because I love you.'

But every time she saw him she knew that he would not have believed her, and at least she was sparing herself that humiliation.

On Saturday the house was full until evening. During the week the auctioneers had made lists of lots, and on Saturday morning the pantechnicon drew up. Sylvia and Laurence hovered around while furniture and packing cases containing small items were loaded aboard to be taken for temporary storage.

Earlier Lucy had looked round her bedroom and decided it could all go to auction. Wherever she went, and whatever happened to her, would be a fresh start, so that when the removal van rolled away her bedroom was the only room in the house that looked more or less the way it had for years.

She went upstairs after waving goodbye to her mother and father and the couple they were staying with. She had been invited along but her mother had said, 'Lucy will be going down to Aunt Maud's,' and Lucy had said, 'Thank you, but I am fixed up.'

She could only stay here another night cr two and then it would have to be Aunt Maud's or some obliging friend. When Matt went it could be Aunt Maud's without any danger. Except that Aunt Maud would be perpetually harking back to Matt, refusing to believe that her matchmaking had come to nothing.

Which it had. Lucy was beginning to accept that. She would have given years of her life to put the clock back a few weeks. Sitting here in this room, she could almost believe that the rest of the house was unaltered, and that she might run down the long hall and open the door and call to Matt. And that he could be waiting for her.

But outside this room everything had changed, and when she came down the stairs now she imagined how it would look as a small hotel. Something rather special, she supposed, and she thought, I wonder if he's got staff lined up. If he needs a receptionist, with secretarial training and handy in the kitchen.

She might work here, stay here; she could keep in touch that way. Because every time she thought, I give up, I shall never get him back, a voice in her blood cried, 'No.'

The statue of the Victorian lady with the basket of fruit still stood in her alcove of hedge waiting for the auction sale, and Lucy strolled across the lawn towards her. 'We're both on offer,' she said, 'and I think you stand a better chance than I do.' Matt had put his hand over the marble hand that first night; now Lucy touched the cold fingers. 'Wish me luck,' she said.

It was a cosy scene in Aunt Maud's parlour. Aunt Maud and Bernard Beddows and another couple were playing a hand of bridge and taking a glass of wine. When Lucy looked in they were preoccupied, although they all smiled at her and Aunt Maud said, 'Oh, hello, dear.'

'Is Matt here?'

'He's in the garden, cleaning up the millstone.'

She expected to find someone else around; she could hardly believe the silence out there. Of late there had always seemed to be eyes watching and ears cocked to every word she said. But this evening she walked over the grass towards the tree and nobody called to her.

Matt was kneeling, scraping the surface of the millstone with a small palette knife. Lichen had peeled away in a pile of green strips, leaving the surface mottled and discoloured, and she said, 'I think I liked it better with whiskers on.'

'Soon grow a new crop.' He was in casual clothes, jeans and open-necked shirt, but she still could not reach him. She sat down on the grass.

'I came to see you about a job, if you do open the house as a hotel.'

'Doing what?' He went on scraping.

'Receptionist? I'm good on a telephone.'

'Very well, if that's how it works out.'

'Can I scrape a bit?' He handed her the palette knife and she eased a little more lichen loose, and babbled about today's removals and that the Victorian statue was going for auction. Unless of course he fancied keeping her as a feature of the gardens.

'Why not?' he said. 'She fits in where she is.'

There was nothing between them but the lightest of talk. The gulf was as wide as ever and she thought, I'm sinking in quicksand here and I can't even cry for help. She dropped the little scrapper and as she stabbed with her thumbnail at a peeling piece of moss inside the ring, she brushed Matt's hand and saw his face.

It whitened beneath the tan. He was holding her hand, their fingers locked, and she stared and saw the mask ripped away and with it every trace of his iron control. In his eyes was such naked appeal that the tears she had held back all week filled her own eyes and she whispered, 'It was the true ring of rock on Strona.'

'It had to be.' He stood up, lifting her, pressing her fingers to his face, and the next moment she was in his arms, clinging to him as if he had dragged her from quicksand. 'Don't cry,' he begged.

'I'm not.' But tears were streaming down her face. They turned away from the house, the windows and possibly the watchers, his arm around her, and she gulped, 'Where are we going?'

'To Strona.'

'All right.'

'Perhaps not tonight.' They went through the gate at the bottom of the gardens and to where his Porsche was parked. By now her mascara was in her eyes and she was blinking and sniffing as he put her into the car and found her a wad of tissues.

She covered her face, mopping frantically, and looked up to see a woman she knew across the road goggling at her. Beside her Matt said, 'What do you think she's making of this?'

Giggles surfaced, catching on the tears, making her cough and then laugh. 'Let's go and tell the lady you want her,' she said.

'That I do.' He kissed her wet cheek and she blotted up the last remnants of eye make-up, pulling down the mirror flap to trace the floating specks.

'I look awful,' she said.

'Not to me.'

He was the one man with whom she would never have to pretend. White-faced and red-eyed, she was still beautiful to him, and even the idiot things she had done didn't matter any more. As they drew up before the dark and empty house, she called across to the pale shape of the statue, 'It's all right. You're safe now.'

'We're all safe now,' said Matt.

She took a key from her pocket, opening the front door, dropping her jacket on a chair. Everything in here was a reject all waiting to be auctioned. In the drawing-room, curtains were drawn at one of the windows. There were still sofas and chairs but darker shapes showed up the faded wallpaper. Pictures and ornaments had been cleared away and it felt as unlived in as a waiting-room. It was here she had lain in Matt's arms. He was remembering too, reading her mind, and he said, 'It isn't lust. It's love as I have never in my life loved anyone else. Let me look at you.' He held her gently. 'When you said "love" and meant Giles it went through me like a knife.' His eyes devoured her and she looked back at him with the same sweet hunger, but for now the touching and the kissing were comfort and reassurance. They were together and savouring the wonder of it.

She said, 'I couldn't have married him. I was scared to phone you in case you said you wouldn't come back, but when I asked Aunt Maud to I didn't know you could buy the house. I thought we might live on Strona. That's how I wanted it to be. Like Strona again.'

'So did I,' he said. 'Oh, God, so did I.'

'In the dark, it was.' They were standing by a window and she reached to pull the heavy brocade curtains close so that hardly any light crept into the room. 'This could be Strona,' she said. 'Why didn't you say you hadn't had Aunt Maud's money? I would have believed you.'

'I heard you talking to her and I thought you'd come and you were going to say you'd finished with Giles. As soon as I saw you I knew you hadn't, and then you accused me of robbing poor old Maud. I could have killed you.' His fingers were on her throat, caressing, his lips kissed the soft beating pulse, and he said, 'No, I couldn't. No way could I ever harm you. But I got out and I was not coming back.' He smiled; she saw that in the darkness. 'And then Maud rang and said you needed me and I came running. Ever since you took off from Strona not a day has passed that I have not thought of you again and again. Not a night when I haven't dreamt of you or lain awake aching for you. When you were outside my door last Saturday night I nearly grabbed you. I would have done if you hadn't jumped away like a scalded cat.'

She flung her head back now, in exasperated laughter. 'You *glared* at me. "You wouldn't be calling on me," you said.' She mimicked his deeper voice, striking an attitude and sending something flying with her elbow.

'Don't smash up the goods,' he said. 'Your old man's counting on them.'

She opened the curtains a crack, switched on a light, and righted the little table she had just knocked over, then sat down on the sofa, slipping off her shoes. 'Actually,' she said, 'when I started down the corridor I was calling on you. But then I panicked and then I ran.'

'Don't run again.'

He sat besides her, an arm around her so that she nestled against him and they both knew her answer, a fervent, 'Oh, I promise I won't.' She asked wistfully, because this was the start of all her heartaches, 'If I hadn't run in the first place, from Strona, what would have happened next?'

'I had that planned.' He was rueful, too, but now they could smile about it. 'I'd selected the food and the wine, the room was ready, champagne and candles. It's an old manor house. I'm proud of it, and I'd hoped you'd take to it.'

'It would have been a lovely evening,' she sighed.

'It will be,' he said. 'We've time to make up for.'

'Aunt Maud will swear she saw it all in her crystal ball.'

'Don't knock Maud. When I asked about you she always said you were well and happy but she never sounded too sure. Then she wrote to tell me you were getting married and sent me that cutting of you, smiling at Alys Lessing's blue-eyed boy, and I had to get down here. Maud will be guest of honour at the wedding in a new pair of gypsy earrings.'

She shifted in the crook of his arm. 'We *are* married.' She took her keeper off her right hand and put it on her left. 'Does that look better?'

'Talking of rings,' he said. 'I nearly smashed that one the Lessings gave you. But right now we're talking of weddings. You know we're married, and I know we're married, but we'd better humour them.'

'I love you,' she said and the dark flame in his eyes was a blaze that dazzled her. She opened her arms and just before he kissed her managed to say, 'This is a horsehair sofa, not very comfortable.'

He finished the kiss, which took a long time and left her limp, then he said, 'Shall we book into a hotel?'

'There's one room upstairs that's not so bad.'

She hadn't had a night's rest in that bed this week. She might not have much rest tonight but the hours of waking would be paradise. Although if she didn't get off this sofa right now she would not get out of this room. 'Yes?' she said.

'Whatever you say.'

As they came into the hall the phone rang. Matt picked it up, listened and offered her the receiver. He went on towards the staircase and she heard Giles's voice. Incredibly, he sounded placatory. Perhaps they had been hasty, he said. The top buttons of her dress were undone and she began unfastening the rest with the phone against her cheek and Giles's voice buzzing in her ears. She said, 'No, you were right, it would never have worked. We didn't love each other,' and cut off the connection. Then she laid the receiver on the table and ran up the stairs, into the lovely dark and Matt's waiting arms.

# ATTRACTIVE, SPACE SAVING BOOK RACK

Display your most prized novels on this handsome and sturdy book rack. The hand-rubbed walnut finish will blend into your library decor with quiet elegance, providing a practical organizer for your favorite hard-or soft-covered books.

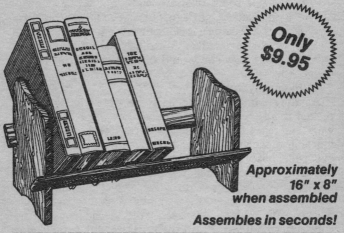

*Only $9.95*

**Approximately 16" x 8" when assembled**

**Assembles in seconds!**

To order, rush your name, address and zip code, along with a check or money order for $10.70* ($9.95 plus 75¢ postage and handling) payable to *Harlequin Reader Service*:

Harlequin Reader Service
Book Rack Offer
901 Fuhrmann Blvd.
P.O. Box 1396
Buffalo, NY 14269-1396

*Offer not available in Canada.*

\* New York and Iowa residents add appropriate sales tax.

BKR-1A

# What readers say about Harlequin romance fiction...

"I absolutely adore Harlequin romances! They are fun and relaxing to read, and each book provides a wonderful escape."
—N.E.,* Pacific Palisades, California

"Harlequin is the best in romantic reading."
—K.G.,* Philadelphia, Pennsylvania

"Harlequins have been my passport to the world. I have been many places without ever leaving my doorstep."
—P.Z.,* Belvedere, Illinois

"My praise for the warmth and adventure your books bring into my life."
—D.F.,* Hicksville, New York

"A pleasant way to relax after a busy day."
—P.W.,* Rector, Arkansas

*Names available on request.

# Six exciting series for you every month... from Harlequin

### *Harlequin Romance*·
### The series that started it all

Tender, captivating and heartwarming...
love stories that sweep you off to faraway places
and delight you with the magic of love.

◆

### *Harlequin Presents*·
### Powerful contemporary love stories...as individual as the women who read them

The No. 1 romance series...
exciting love stories for you, the woman of today...
a rare blend of passion and dramatic realism.

◆

### *Harlequin Superromance*®
### It's more than romance...
### it's Harlequin Superromance

A sophisticated, contemporary romance-fiction
series, providing you with a longer,
more involving read...a richer mix of complex plots,
realism and adventure.

# Harlequin
## *American Romance*™
### Harlequin celebrates the American woman...

...by offering you romance stories written about American women, by American women for American women. This series offers you contemporary romances uniquely North American in flavor and appeal.

◆

## *Harlequin Temptation*™
### Passionate stories for today's woman

An exciting series of sensual, mature stories of love...dilemmas, choices, resolutions... all contemporary issues dealt with in a true-to-life fashion by some of your favorite authors.

◆

## Harlequin Intrigue™
### Because romance can be quite an adventure

Harlequin Intrigue, an innovative series that blends the romance you expect... with the unexpected. Each story has an added element of intrigue that provides a new twist to the Harlequin tradition of romance excellence.

# Harlequin Books®

PROD-A-2